Brave Hearts

Brave Hearts

A San Francisco Story

The Grit and Dreams of an Irish Immigrant Family

Jean Mahoney

Sisters Singing Publishers

For information about permission to reproduce selections of this book, write to:
Permissions, Sisters Singing Publishers, PO Box 5217, Santa Cruz, CA 95063,
or info@sisterssinging.com.

Website: www.sisterssinging.com

Designed by Christy Collins

1 3 5 7 9 10 8 6 4 2
Library of Congress Cataloging in Publication Data
Mahoney, Jean
   Brave hearts: a San Francisco story: the grit and dreams of an Irish immigrant family /
Jean Mahoney. – 1ˢᵗ ed.
   p. cm.
   ISBN 978-0-9845074-1-2

San Francisco (Calif.)—History. 2. Irish-Americans-History. 3. Mahoney, Jean.

Dedication

For my mother
Barbara Mahoney

Barbara Mahoney, age 4,
San Francisco, CA, 1923
(Author Collection)

Family Tree

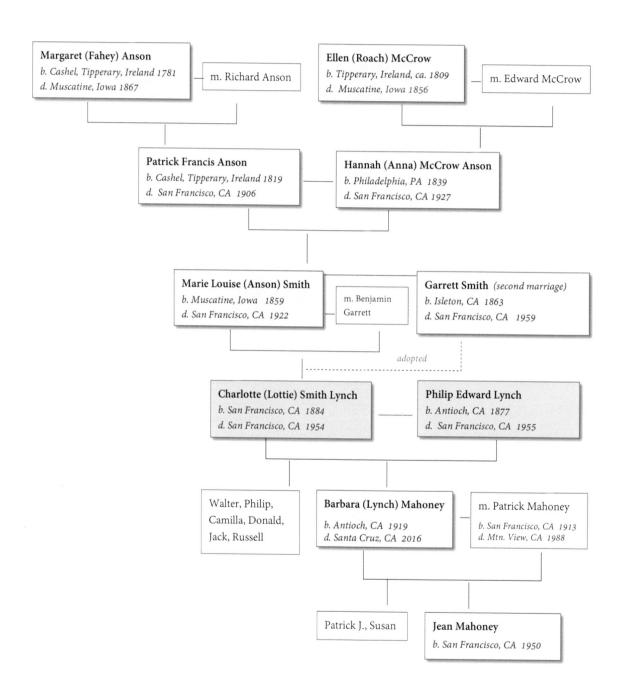

Margaret (Fahey) Anson
b. Cashel, Tipperary, Ireland 1781
d. Muscatine, Iowa 1867

m. Richard Anson

Ellen (Roach) McCrow
b. Tipperary, Ireland, ca. 1809
d. Muscatine, Iowa 1856

m. Edward McCrow

Patrick Francis Anson
b. Cashel, Tipperary, Ireland 1819
d. San Francisco, CA 1906

Hannah (Anna) McCrow Anson
b. Philadelphia, PA 1839
d. San Francisco, CA 1927

Marie Louise (Anson) Smith
b. Muscatine, Iowa 1859
d. San Francisco, CA 1922

m. Benjamin Garrett

Garrett Smith *(second marriage)*
b. Isleton, CA 1863
d. San Francisco, CA 1959

adopted

Charlotte (Lottie) Smith Lynch
b. San Francisco, CA 1884
d. San Francisco, CA 1954

Philip Edward Lynch
b. Antioch, CA 1877
d. San Francisco, CA 1955

Walter, Philip, Camilla, Donald, Jack, Russell

Barbara (Lynch) Mahoney
b. Antioch, CA 1919
d. Santa Cruz, CA 2016

m. Patrick Mahoney
b. San Francisco, CA 1913
d. Mtn. View, CA 1988

Patrick J., Susan

Jean Mahoney
b. San Francisco, CA 1950

Contents

Part Four

Prologue

Do not be fooled. These are people. They are the same as you, as me. Different times. Different climate. Different news. Sometimes from the same town you grew up in. Sometimes not. They worried about their families. They were proud of their children. They had bad days, and good days, and days when they didn't know which end was up. Things went wrong for them, and things went right.

The thing is—these are your people. Whether you are born into this family or not, everyone has people. Sometimes you see life the way they did. You find that you have their eyes, their hair, their hands, that smile of yours. In this book, their names were Margaret and Ellen, Patrick and Anna, Marie Louise and Garrett, Philip and Lottie. Their parents called them home for dinner by those names—just like yours did, just like yours.

And just like you, they had days when they were young when the world was theirs. They could do anything—cross oceans, settle in new lands, look for work, build a house, cut the lumber to make that house—anything. They played hard: skipped rope, played baseball, kick-the-can, hide-and-seek. They hunted for ducks in the Sacramento Delta, pulled water from the wells in Ireland, ran to school, and they rode there on horseback. They learned to read and write, did sums in their heads and on paper. They ran businesses, hauled hay, grain and coal in wagons up and down city streets, sat and held the reins above teams of horses, baled hay, drove their crops to the pier, loaded grain onto barges, then sailed to the City of San Francisco.

They cooked and washed, and cooked and washed, and did it all over again and again and again. They sewed their own wedding dresses, hardly ever bought clothes from a store. They put their hair in pigtails, played tricks on each other, kept dogs as pets, and lived on farms. Later they wore fancy hats with long, colorful feathers. They walked the streets of San Francisco, and they lived through earthquakes, big and small. They held babies until the shaking stopped, and they did rescue work by the Ferry Building.

They had grand parties, learned elocution, recited poems aloud, played the fiddle, danced the jig and the foxtrot, waltzed with their fiancés, listened to the radio, and a couple of them owned a silent movie theater in the 1920s. They laughed until tears ran down their cheeks, and cried sometimes because they missed their folks back in Ireland.

They became Californians—people who knew the redwoods, breathed the salt air and fog of the Pacific Ocean. We breathe the same air, walk the same streets, seek the same refuge in our family and friends. We marvel at how clever we are, strike our foreheads when we get surprised, cry when we're sad. And they got confused by life too, don't be fooled. I want to tell you their stories; they're just people, like you and I, just folks who lived a while ago.

Introduction

Over the years I have been fascinated by the stories my mother, Barbara Mahoney, told me about her parents and grandparents in early San Francisco and the greater Bay Area. We talked about these ancestors so often that one day she suggested I write their stories down. That was ten years ago. Since then I have visited the towns, streets, rivers and addresses where my grandparents and great-grandparents lived. My approach has been to research and write a narrative of their lives, then to bring their stories to life with historical fiction written from their point of view. These stories are based on oral history, genealogical records and intensive research. At the end of this book, I explain for each chapter what I knew when I began each tale. The facts, names, dates and times were made clearer by invaluable records researched and documented by my cousin Nancy Basque, a gifted genealogist who has compiled a veritable treasure trove of files and cabinets of our family's history, starting out as immigrants from Ireland. In addition, there was information from library research, newspapers, and historical photographs, as well as richly documented internet sites with historical records. My family, my mother, brother, sister, uncles and cousins all told me what they knew, and what they had been told by our shared ancestors.

Then the rest was told to me by the ones who have gone before. They gave me the timbre of their voices, their grit, their sorrows, their joys. Their day-to-day ways were made available to me easily because I am one of them. Sometimes I had to ask permission, or get clear on whose voice to use, and see if I had gotten it right. Through this genetic connection of ours, a trust was formed between us—people from my past and myself writing now.

This book is the story of my grandmother Charlotte Smith Lynch's family line, beginning with her first ancestors to come to America from Ireland and following her life and times in San Francisco and the Sacramento Delta. Charlotte, who they called Lottie, was a talented performer and artist. As a young married woman, she lived through the 1906 earthquake and experienced the 1915 Panama-Pacific International Exposition. She saw the Golden Gate Bridge built and the entire region come into its modern form. Her long and full life with my grandfather Philip Lynch is the heart of this book. But we begin with the brave voyagers and immigrants who made Lottie's life in San Francisco possible. Her grandparents, Patrick and Anna Anson, arrived in the City in 1864, when San Francisco was still a newly growing town. Before that, her great-grandparents had sacrificed and suffered to cross the Atlantic to get to American shores. Her Irish-born great-grandmothers, Margaret Anson and Ellen McCrow, lived incredible lives. Margaret Anson was sixty-six years old when she journeyed over the ocean to America in 1847. Ellen McCrow made the rough and dangerous crossing over the ocean as a young woman from County Tipperary, arriving in America in 1837.

Beginning with Margaret and Ellen, there is a long, strong line of women who carried my grandmother Lottie's family forward in America with their perseverance, talents, love of life and wisdom. Their husbands, fathers, and brothers accompanied them and supported their various life decisions. Yet in historical records, these women are often cited as "the wife of..." It was not the custom of their generations to honor them with equal measure. Let us honor them now. They are: my third-great-grandmothers Margaret Fahey Anson and Ellen Roach McCrow; my second-great-grandmother Anna McCrow Anson; my great-grandmother Marie Louise Anson Smith; my grandmother Charlotte Smith Lynch; and my mother Barbara Lynch Mahoney.

My mother told me the stories of these women, and of all her ancestors and their kin. But mostly she told the stories of her parents, Lottie and Philip Lynch, who are the heart of his book. Their beautiful wedding portrait graces the cover, and I knew and loved both of them as a small girl. This book is dedicated to my mother, but it is my grandparents Charlotte and Philip who carry the story, beginning with the women of Charlotte's line dating far back into Ireland.

Charlotte (Lottie) Lynch & Barbara Mahoney, downtown San Francisco, 1930s (Author Collection)

PART ONE
Immigrants & Settlers
1837–1885

CHAPTER 1
For the Hope of It All
1837–1856

My mother attended a San Francisco Giants baseball game every year for forty-eight years in a row, up to the very last year of her life, even hoping to attend the summer of 2016 but she passed away that year, just one month after her ninety-seventh birthday. Before each and every one of those baseball games, all of the fans, herself included, would stand, put their hands over their hearts and sing America's national anthem. The last lines of the anthem are a stirring recollection of what makes us one country, *"The star-spangled banner in triumph shall wave, Oe'r the land of the free and the home of the brave!"*

There is an historical basis for America, a country now made up primarily of immigrants, to feel that it is "the land of the free, and the home of the brave." All of my mother's Irish ancestors came here to be free—free of oppression, free of unending generations of poverty, free to practice their spiritual heritage. Barbara's great-great-grandparents all have different stories, but all of them made one of the bravest acts in their lives when they boarded ships for America. They were brave enough to sail away from Ireland, away from mothers, fathers, friends, siblings, even sometimes spouses and children.

Questions arise from each of these journeys, questions that have factual answers in ships' records, marriage certificates, and census figures. Yet the motives and emotions of these ancestors cannot be reflected in their names on a docket. What *is* known is that by leaving the country of their birth, they decided to take their chances for a better life. And they left forever the difficult futures that loomed in Ireland.

By the time my mother died in 2016, her maternal ancestors had been in the United States for 150 years. Her great-great-grandmother, Margaret Fahey Anson, was born in 1781 in Cashel in County Tipperary. Margaret's village was at the foot of the famous Rock of Cashel, a huge rock outcropping which had once been the royal site of the King of Munster, and later was a thriving medieval monastery with a large cathedral. Margaret's people, the Faheys, were from an ancient Gaelic family that reached back at least a thousand years into old Ireland, to a shining time in Ireland's past.

Yet by the time Margaret was born, the native Irish had suffered from centuries of oppression, poverty and revolt. Ireland had been invaded by the English, and was by then a British colony. Cruel penal laws had been enacted with the goal of eradicating the Catholic faith in Ireland. In the early 1800s, when Margaret Fahey married Richard Anson, they felt the weight of English persecution heavily upon them. They were forbidden to practice their religion openly. They could not publicly speak Irish, their native tongue. With little industry and no jobs available to Catholics, almost all native Irish families relied upon the potato as a subsistence crop, and lived from season to season in cottages built by hand from stones dug from the earth. It is likely that Margaret and Richard were tenant farmers who had the tenancy passed down to them, but had no hope of ever owning the land on which they lived and worked. They tried to eke out a living on their homeland's soil as tenant farmers under English landlords' rules.

Margaret and Richard bore their first son, my grandmother Charlotte's grandfather Patrick Anson, in 1819. Patrick would grow up to fight in America's Civil War and lived out his life in San Francisco—a future that none of them could have remotely imagined when he was born in the poor village of Cashel, Ireland. Over the next few years, Margaret and Richard had three more sons and one daughter. As the children grew, persecution only continued, and poverty increased. Still, Margaret and Richard made sure their children

Rock of Cashel, early 1830s, with ancient cathedral and peasant cottages (J. Stirling Coyne, *The Scenery and Antiquities of Ireland*, 2004)

were educated. The boys learned to read, write, and mastered arithmetic, which they used all throughout their lives in America. It is likely that they attended "hedge schools" in Cashel set up by Jesuit priests to educate Catholic children. The "hedge schools" were hidden schools, oftentimes in the countryside, hidden in hedges, away from English magistrates' sights.

Margaret and Richard began to dream of a new life in America, and when Patrick turned twenty-four years old, he struck out for a better future by emigrating. It would have been a huge effort for the family to save the ship's fare, probably over several years. It appears that the goal from the start was to bring the rest of the family to join him after he found work, for the rest followed soon after.

Patrick's journey across the rough Atlantic Ocean took six weeks. In 1843, conditions on ships crossing the ocean were incredibly difficult, particularly in steerage class. The ships were often poorly built, crowded, disease-ridden, and short of food, supplies and medical services. As a result, many Irish immigrants contracted diseases such as typhus, and many died before reaching land. So bad were these ocean crossings that ships during this time were often called "coffin ships." It was brave for any immigrant in the 1840s even to step foot on one, to throw their fate into the winds of hope.

But Patrick did arrive, landing in Nova Scotia, Canada in August 1843, after sailing on the ship the *North America*. He made his way to Boston, where he settled for a time, working as a house painter. However, in the 1840s, Irish-Catholic immigrants were unwelcome in Boston. Patrick encountered notices declaring "No Irish Need Apply" and ultimately moved farther west to St. Louis, Missouri, where anti-Irish discrimination was not so engrained. Patrick worked hard and he saved money. In only a few years, he was able to send enough funds back to Ireland to purchase ship's passage for his three brothers, Richard, Lawrence and Michael, as well as his sister Mary and his sixty-nine-year-old mother Margaret, to sail to America. His father Richard had died in the years after Patrick left Ireland.

To reunite the family was an incredible feat—made even more difficult because it was accomplished during Ireland's terrible tragedy, the Great Famine. The Famine began two years after Patrick left for America, and lasted from 1845 to 1850, due to the failure of Ireland's potato crop. The Famine, known in Ireland as

"Destitution in Ireland-failure of the potato crop"
(*London Pictorial Times*, 22 August 1846)

the "Great Hunger," brought starvation, death and extreme illness throughout Ireland. When Margaret Anson left her homeland with her sons and daughter in 1847, it was under the most horrific of circumstances. In those five years, two million of her fellow Irish died, hundreds if not thousands right around her and her family in Cashel. Still another two million Irish did as she and her family did, and sailed away. They went to America, to Australia, to England and to other ports where they could lead better lives.

Margaret's daughter, Mary, and her son, Michael, sailed into New Orleans in 1847 on the American steamship *Washington,* to be joined soon by their mother and siblings. Then Margaret and two of her sons, Richard and Lawrence, also landed in the Port of New Orleans and boarded a riverboat to sail up the Mississippi River to join Patrick in St. Louis around 1847. Each fare for the crossing was about 40 shillings, or $10 each for steerage class. By 1850, the Anson family were all reunited and living in St. Louis. It must have been incredible for Margaret to sail up the river, taking in the new land where she had set her hopes for a better life for her and her children.

Margaret Fahey Anson
~1850~

Leaving me homeland was a true test of me faith. I saw families in Cashel dying all around us, may their souls all rest in peace. The potatoes we depended upon for our daily survival just died on the vine from blight, and famine ravaged the villages. Both young and old died from starvation. Me four boys, my daughter and meself left out to America while we were still alive. Me husband Richard was already gone to an early grave, and I knew me family had no hope anymore in me homeland. So we boarded the ship and sailed away. For the hope of it all, don't you see?

Back in those awful years, we Irish had a saying, "There's hope from the sea, but there's no hope from the grave." I saw me dear husband die the year before I left me homeland forever. Me firstborn son, Patrick, was safe in America, in a place called St. Louis. Just knowing Patrick was safe and thriving, with money he'd saved to send back to us for our passage, was enough to steel meself away, and just let Ireland go. I left me homeland of almost seventy years to live out the rest of me life in the far away country of America. I sailed for me own life, for me family's future. Me sons and me daughter were all I had. What future did I have to look forward to, you see? I needed to live where we could work, eat, and be free of starvation and poverty.

'Course if you do the math, you see I was one of the oldest immigrants on the ship. At sixty-six I was in good health and had escaped! The voyage took forty-nine days and we went in the lowest part of the ship, called steerage. It was a rough trip, but I arrived on America's shores to begin the next chapters in the book of me life. And although I left a teary goodbye at me husband's grave, I knew he would want me to live and see our children be well.

We arrived in America at the Port of New Orleans, then sailed up the long Mississippi to arrive in St Louis, Missouri. To be sure, I took in the differences between this new county and me home village of Cashel. America was as Patrick's letters told us, but no one could imagine without seein' it all—the great steamships, the towns set right upon the river, the great brick two- and three-story buildings and smokestacks. There were soft hills, and the river was wide and long like our Shannon, but the towns and factories had me eyes wide.

But the real difference between the two was that was, well, first of all there was no starvation. There were many other things bein' different to me, of course. The land in St. Louis was green, but 'twas not so green as me homeland. St. Louis was busy, with busy roads and lots of buildings, more built every day. I took a deep breath and went forward. The land in America had gotten rain but I was missing the Irish constant soft rain. The rainbows here were few and far between, but at this point in me life, I didn't mind, because, you see, I *had* life. I had me children, and we had life, and we had food. The blessing of it was food, and land to own ourselves. Of course, the best of it all was to be together again. To see my Patrick again, strong and well in America. But the best of it all, the blessing of life, was enough food.

After the Ansons were reunited in America, for a time they all lived together in St. Louis, Missouri. Sadly, Margaret's daughter Mary died a few years after they arrived due to "ship fever," likely a lingering sickness contracted on board. But Margaret herself was hardy and strong. She lived on, and her sons Patrick, Michael, Lawrence and Richard found work as painters and glaziers (window installers). Margaret kept house for them, knowing that her choice to immigrate had made it possible to witness her sons make new lives and build prosperity. The Anson family's names can be found in city directories of St Louis of that time.

After a few years, one of the younger sons, Richard, decided to explore America. He sailed down the Mississippi to Louisiana, where he met and married a widow with two children. Richard ultimately took his new family all the way to San Francisco, becoming the first to reach the American far west. He settled permanently in San Francisco, where he and his wife Mary raised five boys.

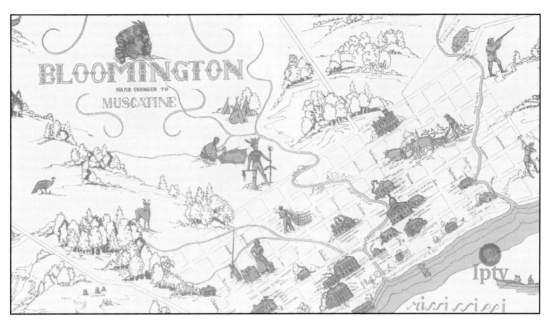

Historic map of Muscatine, name changed from Bloomington in 1849 (Musser Public Library, Muscatine, Iowa)

Back in St. Louis, immigrants and new settlers continued to arrive, and competition for jobs and housing increased. After two years, the rest of the Anson family decided to sail up the Mississippi River to the new small town of Muscatine, Iowa. When they arrived in 1852, there were 2,000 Muscatine residents. Major William Williams, a visitor at the time, described Muscatine as having "many neat residences and several spacious brick mercantile establishments: a large steam mill, one smaller one, two printing establishments, 6 churches, 4 physicians, 8 lawyers, a neat court house and jail, Masonic lodge, etc.... This town is very prettily situated, in part on a level on the river for two streets back...All steamboats land here, passing up and down."

It was in the young town of Muscatine that Margaret Anson and her sons would put down roots and settle. They found other Catholic families who joined together to celebrate Mass on the occasional Sunday when a travelling prairie priest, Father Mazzuchelli, came to town. To their delight, they discovered other Irish immigrants from their own County Tipperary. Among these friendship ties was a fateful connection with John Roach and his sister Ellen McCrow. Ellen was forty years old, with several growing children, and had lived in Muscatine since its inception ten years before. In this small town and within the even smaller Irish-Catholic community, Margaret and Ellen made a connection. As fate would have it, the bonds between their children Patrick and Anna would create my grandmother Lottie's ancestral line.

Ellen McCrow was the first of my grandmother Lottie's ancestors to leave Ireland for American shores. She was born in Tipperary, and left Ireland in 1837, in the 26th year of her life, sailing from Ireland to Liverpool, then from Port of Liverpool to America on the ship *Oconee*. She arrived several weeks later in Philadelphia, on April 10, with two brothers and one sister. Ellen traveled under her maiden name of Roach. She was on the ship's manifest as a spinster. Her brother, William Roach, age 24, was listed as a peddler; John Roach was listed as a 21-year-old laborer, and Ellen's sister, Brigit Roach, age 18, was also listed as a spinster. The word "spinster" at that time often referred to a female's occupation of spinner as well as an unmarried woman. Their older brother Thomas Roach was already in America two years past, and may have sent the ten schillings passage fare for each of his siblings to travel all at once.

All four siblings were listed under the surname Roach, but historical records show that Ellen had another last name, the name of Lacey. Ellen had been married back in Ireland, and when she left, she had to leave behind three young children, aged twelve, eleven and nine years old. She sailed to America to make a new life, on new shores, as a new woman. Questions that are unanswerable arise, a myriad of questions as to why Ellen would leave her three children and her extended family to travel so far and away.

We do not know the circumstances of her marriage—whether she was widowed, divorced or abandoned—only that Ellen bore her first child at sixteen years old. Yet somehow her marriage ended, and her life in Ireland as young Irish-Catholic mother with three children was beyond harsh. When she left Ireland in 1837, the country was afflicted with widespread poverty. There was no hope for a real future in her homeland with the extreme prejudice against her Catholic faith. It seemed at every turn she faced unanswerable challenges. As a single mother, she had to find a way to create security and safety for herself and her children. After her marriage ended, she may have returned to live with her parents in the Roach family homestead.

Ultimately, she arranged for her children to stay behind in Ireland, cared for by her parents or a close relative, and counted herself in for the long, forty-five-day voyage to America in steerage class. Her brother Thomas had gone on ahead, just as Patrick Anson would do a few years later for his own family. The Roach siblings relied on their brother Thomas's encouraging letters with tales of a life free from poverty and oppression.

This voyage must have been one of the hardest decisions of Ellen's life. She could only hope that the plan she made to see her three Irish-born children again in America would somehow come to fruition.

Ellen Roach McCrow
~1837~

Yes, yes indeed, leaving Michael, Julia and little Mary in Ireland with my mum and dad was the hardest decision I ever had to make. But, you see, I did it for them. After seeing Ireland the way it was back then, I knew they wouldn't have a future. And I knew that Thomas, being our oldest, most trusted brother, was truly a hard worker and a kind man. We believed his letters from America. Clasped them to our breasts, my brothers, sister and I, as our only hope. I had faith that my parents would watch over my three safely. And I set off. I set off with the hope and faith that had been my rock ever since I was a young girl. The Church gave me solace over the years. I prayed every day to find work in America fast. I was young and strong at just twenty-six years of age and I prayed that my body and wits would carry me through to the day that my three children would arrive in America, safe, strong and free from all our troubles.

When my brothers and I arrived in Philadelphia on that tenth day of April in 1837, we were exhausted from the voyage, but arrived healthy and got our confidence about us soon after. We all found work. I went to work in the mills as a spinner. After one year there, I met and married Edward McCrow, a Protestant. He was a good man, just twenty years old, but smart, energetic and ambitious, and he loved me. He was himself just arrived from Ireland. Edward and I had one daughter in Philadelphia: Hannah Jane, born on March 1, 1839.

After three years in Philadelphia, Edward and I began to realize that America was a vast country with more towns and opportunities for us ahead. There were strikes at the mills where we worked, and the tenements where we lived were getting too crowded for our growing family. We heard about a new town called Bloomington in the state of Iowa, way out west, located on the Mississippi River. Edward wanted to own land, so we moved almost 1,000 miles, travelling by wagons and boats along the waterways. I was pregnant at the time with our second daughter, and the journey was long, arduous and successful! We arrived and our little Ellen was born just after, in April of 1841. Now we had two American-born daughters. Yet do not think that there was a day gone by that I didn't pine for and hope that my three in Ireland were well. I wrote to them all the time, and I did pray to see my three Irish-born children soon.

My husband Edward was a hard worker and an excellent provider. He made enough and saved his wages from his work in the Philadelphia mills for our family to buy several small parcels of real estate in Bloomington, which had now changed its name to Muscatine. We finally were settled quite happily. Edward established a successful business as a cobbler, and we were soon established settlers of this young town. Seven years after we arrived in Muscatine, our third daughter Kate was born.

Yet the news at that time from Ireland was dire. Famine was ravishing the villages. I'd never lost touch with my family there and my three dear children, Mary, Michael and Julia. Edward and I finally saved enough money to send for them to sail to America. Praise be and thank God! They arrived in America just as I'd hoped and prayed. Mary, then twenty years old, came first with her husband Patrick and infant son John, coming into New Orleans,

Louisiana in 1847—the worst year of the Famine. They survived the crossing and sailed up the Mississippi River to settle here in Muscatine. Mary's family lived right next door to Edward and me and our three growing girls Hannah, Ellen and little Kate. It was the fulfillment of all I had ever wished for and dreamed, and the happiest time of my life.

My son Michael came from Ireland two years later, in 1849, and lived a long life in Illinois with his wife and children. Julia, my youngest daughter in Ireland, came to America as well and lived in Philadelphia. Now my heart was calm and I was proud that my first three children had all made it here to this new land. Thanks be to God! All three had escaped the terrible Irish Famine.

During the years of 1847 to 1850, I was reunited and living happily with my family, which now consisted of my husband Edward and our three young daughters, Hannah, Ellen and Kate, my Mary, and her husband Michael, now with their own three sons. All of my children were safe and living solid lives in America. They had enough food, and good homes. My life was finally as I hoped. My husband was able to buy and own land. I could worship openly as a Catholic. Our house on Cedar Street in Muscatine held family celebrations, and even a Catholic Mass was celebrated there by the eight Catholic families residing in the new small town, the lovely Anson family from Ireland among them.

In my bones, I was satisfied that my choice to sail here to America was exactly the right one. Oh, we had struggles in America, but Ireland had no food for us, no land to own. If Edward, my brothers and I had stayed there, who knows what our stories would be? America held us well. Our peace in Muscatine lasted for three happy years.

Then, all of a sudden, my family's story turned into tragedy that I could hardly believe. Everything took turns for the worse! The security we all felt vanished when the disease of cholera arrived in Muscatine. That terrible disease took the lives of more than half of my clan. Illness invaded our family and death kept knocking. My heart broke into pieces with each passing. What I would give to take back that terrible week in July of 1850!

The first victims were my dear daughter Mary, who had been living next door to me, and her husband Patrick and two of their three sons. In the end, cholera took four of the five of their family. Mary, Patrick and their five-year-old son John all died on the same awful day, July 12, 1850. Then cholera came to my house and my dear husband Edward took ill and died. What a black grief it was to lose him, and he still strong and in his prime. My three daughters Hannah, Ellen and Kate did not contract the illness, praise be to God, but the scourge would not quit until it also claimed Mary's son, three-year-old Anthony, on July 18. To think of it—my Mary's brood had been a thriving family of five, and now it was reduced to just one, their last son, one-year-old Michael, who somehow survived and was now mine to care for, though all I could do was weep.

All told, cholera took forty in our town of Muscatine in that one week, and it was so quick! I'd always kept a clean house and my daughter Mary did as well. I do not know and will never fully realize what awful fate let that disease into our households. Did the disease come through the town wells? Did it linger from the ship voyage from Ireland? You cannot ask yourself these questions too often. I will never know the answers, but the truth of it is that my family was taken too soon. Why, in just the one day most all of Mary's family gone! Now I was a widow, left on my own without my strong, dependable husband. Perhaps the cholera came from the water we drank in the common wells here. The water in Ireland never made us sick, but I heard cholera killed folks too quickly there as well, during the starving times. I came to America for a better life, and welcomed my daughter here for the same, but to see them all gone in one week and my husband as well, it broke me deep in my soul, and I was not really well or the same ever since.

But I had to carry on. Be with my three daughters: Hannah only eleven, Ellen nine, and Kate two years old, and my grandson Michael, just one year old. I came to see that all of us were spared for a reason. Still my heartbreak took me down, and I had too many, many sleepless nights. But the light of day beckoned me to call upon my strength, and call upon God to accompany me for my daughters and my young grandson. Fortunately, my brother John stepped in and helped me with finances and the running of our family's real estate holdings. John helped collect the rents on our properties so we could have money coming in. I had only a little reading and writing, though I made sure my daughters were well-educated. Married women were not allowed to own title to property, as was the custom of the time. So I was glad John stepped in to help us manage money and property in our time of need. My mind was sharp, but my spirits needed shoring up. The girls and I got through this time, but that one week in July of 1850 weighed too heavily on me the rest of my life.

My brother John did well taking care of our finances and such. But then as fate would have it, my dear brother passed on five years later, in 1855, leaving all his property to me. A reliable friend of ours was an Irishman named Patrick Anson from Cashel in County Tipperary, and we decided to have Patrick appointed as the administrator of the estate. These included the real estate and holdings that my family had, and any business holdings my brother John had.

After John's passing, during that year of 1855, I kept an eye on Patrick Anson. He was a kind, well-educated and trustworthy man, and he really became a lifesaver and family to us. He was a stalwart, dependable fellow. I thought that if anything ever happened to take me too soon from this life, Patrick could be an able guardian for my brood. I knew I wasn't well, and spoke to him about this, asking him to look out for my family if anything ever happened to me. He looked me in the eye and promised that he would. That good, able man, through thick and thin, did exactly as he promised.

Just one year after her brother's passing, Ellen Roach McCrow, my third-great-grandmother, died in 1856, at the age of only forty-seven. The church records of St. Matthias Catholic Church state that she died of a protracted consumptive illness. The stresses of the past six years of her life left Ellen vulnerable and weakened her body. She is buried in St. Mary's Cemetery in Muscatine, Iowa.

At the end of her life, Ellen included all of her children in her will, leaving "her estate both real and personal of any and every kind to my children: Michael Lacey, Julia Stewart, Hannah McCrow, Ellen McCrow, Catherine McCrow and my grandchild Michael Maher." Ellen's first American-born daughter, Hannah (later called Anna), was seventeen when her mother died. By then she had seen too much of life and death. She likely had assumed responsibility of running the McCrow household during the last years of her mother's life. However, Hannah was still a minor, and was now responsible for her sisters, Ellen, who was fifteen, and Kate just eight. All three girls needed a legal guardian. They had been orphaned with no father or mother. Patrick Anson, friend of the family and administrator of their Uncle John's will, was now familiar to them all. Her mother Ellen had already spoken to her of this plan to call on Patrick to be appointed Ellen's daughters' guardian. Patrick, then thirty-eight years old, was willing and able to fill this important role as guardian for the three McCrow daughters. Hannah wrote a letter to Judge Meason requesting the appointment of Patrick F. Anson to become legal guardian. The request was granted in 1856. This was a very wise choice on both Hannah and Patrick's part, and would lead to fates that neither of them could ever imagine.

Signature of Patrick F. Anson, probate document for guardianship of Hannah and sisters, 1856 (Private Collection, Nancy Basque)

CHAPTER 2
Patrick, Anna and the Civil War
1856–1863

At the end of the difficult summer of Ellen's death, Patrick Anson accompanied the three McCrow girls to St. Joseph's Academy boarding school in Dubuque, Iowa. It was just two months after their mother's death, and arrangements had been made for the McCrow siblings to attend boarding school. They had always been well-educated, and Hannah in particular liked to write and read the newspapers and magazines of the day. Patrick kept meticulous financial records of the years the McCrow girls were in his guardianship, which can be found in the records he kept for their expenses. He began by keeping a ledger of their train trip to boarding school in August of 1856. Each item he needed to buy was recorded in neat handwriting. Everything from hair ribbons (26 cents) to train tickets ($9.75 each for Hannah and Ellen $5.45 for Kate) to the school's boarding fees (one year, 3 students, $426.85). Patrick wanted to make sure to avoid any question of impropriety and he took his appointment as guardian very seriously. He would be reimbursed by their estate for these expenses.

The three McCrow sisters only spent one year at St. Joseph's, and did not return to that school. Perhaps it was too hard for the three girls to feel so far from their friends and what family was left in Muscatine. Patrick met them at St. Joseph's in May of 1857 and the group took a steamboat down the Mississippi River to get back home to Muscatine. When the three girls returned, they

16

lived with Patrick's married brother Michael and his wife, along with Patrick's mother Margaret. Patrick continued on as guardian for another year. Hannah soon turned eighteen and came of legal age, and after a time, Patrick petitioned the court to resign his guardianship in April of 1858.

Fate had something else in mind for young Hannah and the helpful Patrick. They fell in love, and married in 1858, when he was thirty-nine and she nineteen. Hannah began formally using the name Anna at the time of her marriage. Patrick's mother Margaret, then eighty years old, was the family matriarch and living with the McCrow girls. She knew that Anna was a solid, intelligent and kind young woman.

Margaret Fahey Anson
~1858~

To be sure, I was glad and relieved that me Patrick had found himself a good wife. I knew Anna McCrow from the time she was a girl in Muscatine, of course. I felt the heartbreak of her family's story, how the sickness took them one by one, all in less than one month's time! First it was the cholera robbin' five of them of the chance of a full life, then Ellen passed on six years later, leaving the three McCrow girls orphans. When Patrick told me he would take on the job of their guardian, I prayed for him. Prayed for him to gather the strength to see these young ones into their adulthood. Of course, Patrick had always done well in school and loved to keep meticulous records of all his earnings and spending.

Margaret Anson, circa 1858 (Musser Public Library, Muscatine, Iowa)

Then, when he returned from that journey, I could see he missed the girls. The nine months while they were away at school passed too slowly for him. He picked them up at St. Joseph's and sure enough, they had decided to all come home to Muscatine and stay. It wasn't long before I could tell that Anna and Patrick were getting a bit of a twinkle in their eyes. I prayed that this marriage would be blessed and happy. After me morning prayers and over me morning tea, I looked up to the heavens for the strength of St. Brigid and St. Patrick to be with all my children. Praise God! I am blessed with a long life, and most of my children alive and prospering here in America. What stories we all have. Yes, praise God, what stories we all have.

My third-great-grandmother Margaret Anson lived the rest of her life in Muscatine, Iowa, and died in 1867 at the age of eighty-six years. She is buried in Muscatine in St. Mary's Cemetery. After her journey across the seas at sixty-six years old, she lived another twenty years in America. She was one of the elders who consoled Anna McCrow and her sisters when they lost their father, and later their mother. When Margaret Anson died, her new daughter-in-law Anna McCrow Anson would remember her mother-in-law's good, long life, and know that her husband came from solid, long-lived stock.

Anna McCrow Anson
~1858~

Patrick and I spent the first years of our marriage peacefully settled in Muscatine. We felt right together from the first. It seemed I had known him all my life, and I could see that Patrick was a good choice. I felt so alone and confused when Mother died. I was just seventeen, my sister Ellen fifteen, and young Kate only eight. I was beside myself with the heartache of it all. It felt like I would have to care for my two sisters alone. That thought was almost too much to bear. I saw that mother took Patrick into her confidence when she was ill. I knew my mother was brave, strong and smart. Since Mother accepted Patrick, it became clear in my mind that he would be our best hope for a guardian if she passed away too soon. If Mother trusted him, so could we.

After Mother was laid to rest, though Patrick was a busy man, I saw how he showed care and kindness to the three of us, just one month later on our train trip out to St. Joseph's Boarding School. He wrote down every expense, helped keep my sisters in line and entertained us all with jokes and stories. I must tell you that during my year at boarding school, I pined for Muscatine and the security that my sisters and I felt there. I was so glad to return to my hometown after that year away. It was twelve months after our return from St. Joseph's that Patrick and I decided to marry. I changed my name then, from Hannah to Anna. I wanted to leave behind all my hard years and start life fresh. So I became Mrs. Anna Anson on May 18, 1858, in St. Mathias Catholic Church in our town of Muscatine.

Patrick and I set up our household and started our family. Our beautiful first daughter Marie Louise was born on April 22, 1859. We were blessed with another healthy daughter Margaret on October 18, 1861. Earlier that same year, we faced a great challenge, as did all the others living in Iowa and the rest of the United States. The Civil War broke out across the land on April 12, 1861. The governor of our state sent his first proclamation to call for the men of Iowa to do their part to register in the Union Army, following President Lincoln's first orders for troops. I cautioned Patrick on enlisting. I'd already seen both my parents gone and didn't want to risk my new husband being killed in this war. Yet the war between the states did not end quickly; it raged on. After two years, more troops were needed and Iowa's governor sent out a second call for soldiers to enlist.

Patrick Anson
~1858~

My feelings for young Hannah McCrow surprised me as much as anyone, and grew slowly over a few years. I saw what an excellent daughter she was, and I knew she had stood strong and helped her mother Ellen after her father's sudden death. The loss was so much for poor Ellen to bear, but Hannah had a strong heart and a calm disposition. She always seemed older than her years. Life had forced her into heartbreak and responsibilities too young, but she kept a cheerful outlook. She had a determination to keep on with life, to find happiness for her mother and for her young sisters.

After her mother died, grief overcame Hannah and her sisters for a time. I was happy to accept the request to serve as their guardian. Then Hannah turned eighteen, and the feelings between us began to change. I knew her so well; she was beautiful, young and strong, and I found I couldn't imagine a better wife and mother of my children. To my joy, she felt the same way. We set up household in Muscatine, and when our first daughter Marie Louise was born, I fought to kept tears back until I was out of sight of Hannah and the midwife. My true life in America had begun.

I could not have imagined then what would come to pass just a few years later. My adopted country, to which I had solemnly pledged allegiance in 1851 when I became a citizen, fell into a Civil War. When I answered my country's call, I had a wife and two young daughters. Still I enlisted and chose to fight for the nine months' term. I was forty-three years old, fit and ready to do my part. In my boyhood in Ireland, I'd felt the boot of the English upon my family, and so I left my homeland for freedom. I felt I had to do my duty to America and defend a man's right to liberty. Here in America everyone was supposed to be free. I met free Negro men and women in Iowa. When they arrived across the border from Missouri, I knew they had been slaves and found their way to freedom by escaping unthinkable cruelties. I heard tell that one of Muscatine's barbers, Alexander Clark, helped runaway slaves. I knew that many of our southern states relied on the work of the Negro slaves, but I knew in my bones that no man should be enslaved. These folks who came to Iowa were looking for a better life, like I did when I left Ireland almost twenty years before.

Because I was one of the older men in the company, I got elected by the men to be an officer in the Iowa East 35th regiment as second lieutenant. In my nine-month campaign, we fought alongside General Sherman and were part of the Battle of Vicksburg. Oh Lord, there are hardly words to tell of this brutal war and its battles! As God is my witness, the sights and sounds of it haunted me over the rest of my life. Hand to hand combat. It was man-to-man rifles and bayonets direct to the body. I saw legions of fallen soldiers left on the field, bleeding and in agony. My heart went out to all my men. I did what I could to lead them, all the while I prayed to get home where my wife and daughters waited for me. I needed to survive. And survive I did.

During those nine months, I saw enough of war to last my lifetime. The sights, sounds and smells of war were almost too much to witness. I saw some of my own men falling in front of my eyes, either severely wounded or dead. When the 35th Iowa East joined the rest of the Union soldiers there in Vicksburg to free that port from the rebels, we emerged victorious. Now I knew that the Battle of Vicksburg was almost over. I saw that our Union Army could open up passage on the Mississippi River. My wife and daughters and I could be free to travel on the big river once again. While I was away at war, during the long, wet, lonely nights, I'd been thinking. My brother Richard had moved far off to San Francisco. It was a faraway dream to go join him. But now I had narrowly missed falling by a bayonet myself. I wrote to Anna that perhaps we should consider the invitation from Richard to join him and his family in San Francisco.

I figured I'd already sailed once in my life to change the way things were going, and now I'd do it again. We could move further out west than I ever thought I would. And this time I'd take Anna, and our daughters Marie Louise and Ellen. That was what I was thinking as my release from my unit came through, an honorable discharge. I sailed up the Mississippi, it was all clear, and met my lovely young family. All three were waiting there in Muscatine, waiting, praying for my return. I scooped up Anna and the girls and breathed my first sigh of relief in nine months.

Anna McCrow Anson
1863

Nine months. I had carried two babies to full term before this war. Each had journeyed nine months inside me, and now Patrick had been gone nine months with the fighting. Fighting for the Union Side. He promised me he'd return, but how could I be sure with the news of battles of raging south of the Mississippi? "Lord," I prayed every day, "Lord, let him live. Let him live. Let him come back home." I put my faith to the test once more, and hoped to see my dear husband alive and well back home.

I was proud of Patrick. We kept up communication as best we could during those nine months. We wrote letters back and forth while he was away. He wrote to me from the battlefields, and I penned my letters at home. His were sporadic, arriving to our home in Muscatine, sometimes one a month with the postmark reading "Soldier's Letter." I wrote when I could find the time between babies and addressed it to Lieutenant Patrick Anson, Iowa's 35th, hoping each missive would find its way into the Confederate States where his unit was marching, following the lead of General Sherman in Louisiana and Mississippi. When I received and read the letters written in his steady hand, I could see confidence in the words. Yet from reading between the lines, talk in town and newspaper accounts, I knew that war, this Civil War, was horrible.

My only means of news and hope were letters, and when one arrived stamped from Vicksburg, dated June 18, 1863, I clasped it to my heart and tucked it away for safekeeping until the news it contained came true. Patrick's resignation had come through! He would return home, making the trip upriver soon. In that summer of 1863, Patrick

Muscatine, circa 1850s, Henry Lewis lithograph (Muscatine Art Center)

indeed sailed up the Mississippi River to Muscatine and arrived home, to my joy for him to hold me and our two daughters Marie Louise and Margaret. He never let go of us again.

CHAPTER 3
City by the Bay
1864-1866

During the years that Patrick's brother, Richard, was living in San Francisco, he had often urged his family to come out west. By the 1860s, San Francisco had become a metropolis with a population of over 56,000 people, an increase from 1848, the year before the Gold Rush, when the population had been 850! It was a vibrant city with all types of immigrants from many parts of the world.

When Richard wanted to tell his older brother Patrick about how good life was in San Francisco, he would have taken out paper, pen, and an inkwell, and written him a letter. Letters in those days took about ten days to cross the country by Pony Express, stagecoach or train. There were no telephones back then, no cell phones, computers or internet, so people hand-wrote letters to one another. People back then took great pride in having good penmanship that was clear and easy to read.

909 Geary Street
San Francisco, California

February 4, 1864

My Dear Brother Pat,

I hope this letter finds you, Anna, and your two girls in good health. I am sure you and your family are doing fine now. They all must be so happy to have you home and safe, as am I. Your letter did reach me last month. We are indeed relieved that your nine months' enlistment as a Civil War lieutenant is over! And once again, I plead with you my brother, gather up your growing family and come to California! Spring will be the best time to travel and sail out West to set your sights on the waters of San Francisco Bay, and the Golden Gate where the Pacific Ocean opens up into the City's ports and beyond. I suggest you choose to sail as we did down the Mississippi to the Gulf, round the Great Cape Horn of Peru, and up the Pacific Coast—all together a journey of about three months.

Patrick, it's beautiful here. The weather in our fair city these last five weeks has been delightful, pleasant and warm. As I write, the boys are in front, trying their hand at stickball. The sun is still shining and some days it's been 70 degrees right here at the beach. And this is only February! Right now, this afternoon, as I look out our bay window I see the barges in the Bay traveling up and down from the Sacramento River hauling fruit, vegetables, coal, hay, and grain, all bound for this city of prosperity. The plum trees in the orchards south of here are blossoming with the sure promise of a good harvest.

Now don't get me wrong, Pat, it did rain, buckets full this fall and early winter. So we know we are well stocked for water in the creeks and lakes. 'Tis for sure the wells won't run dry this summer.

Just this past September, I've taken a job as a painter in addition to my work in the store. There are lots of Victorian type houses being built here in the hillsides, so you will be able to get steady work in town painting them. I have been busy ever since I arrived. I cannot tell you how happy Mary and I both are here in this warm, friendly town with our young ones. When we came to America, this is the land I dreamed of when I was so young, following your example and sailing to this new continent all the way from Ireland way back in '47. Now we're settled in this city and these past fifteen years have given me a sense of the town. We can get you settled with no trouble at all. There's plenty of work for painters like us, with new houses going up all the time.

I tell you Pat, the people are good here. There's little of that "No Irish Need Apply" business here in California. There are lots of jobs, not so much gold anymore to be dug out though, so quite a few of those 49ers, the gold-seekers you heard about in my first letters, have bought farms along the rivers or live in the City here. We are settling in. I will say that San Francisco has its characters—it's not your normal town. A few miles from here there's the Barbary Coast for all the wild ones still sowing their oats. But for us family men like you and me now, we live in respectable neighborhoods and it's grand.

I will close now after this long tome. I have enclosed a postcard of our city by the bay. Please consider your younger brother's plea, Pat, and come out West this spring. You will never be happier.

Your Loving Brother,
Richard

Postcard, "Vista de San-Francisco," Isidore-Laurent Deroy, lithographer, 1860 (Library of Congress)

Anna and Patrick
~Muscatine, Late February 1864~

Anna Anson gratefully read the return address on the front of the envelope that had arrived in the morning's mail. *Ah,* she thought, *another letter from Richard, way out in San Francisco. I hope this will give us just the confidence we need to sail west, where it's warm and I can finally get a glimpse of the blue ocean's waters.* She took out her letter opener, getting ready to present the letter to Patrick. He had just returned from a long day of painting Mrs. Flynn's front parlor in Muscatine. What with more snow about to fall, Patrick found the cold start to settle in his bones. He too longed for a new life. After almost a year as an officer in the Civil War, the things he had seen had drained him of his usual optimism.

He felt torn apart and worse than ever. He turned his attention to his wife, who at that moment was holding a letter.

"You received another letter from Richard, Pat."

"Let me read it straightaway, darlin'." Patrick sat down, shaking his head as he read. This wasn't the first such letter from Richard, suggesting he move to San Francisco, and by God, both he and Anna had been thinking it over with some seriousness these past few months. There was a postcard along with the letter that showed a beautiful new city by a grand bay.

"Well, he's telling me now that it's 70 degrees there in California! Look at this picture postcard. I just don't know, he was always makin' up tales, even when we were younger. I would love to live where we weren't cold all the time, Anna."

"All my life, when the winter comes," Anna said, "I long for the spring. I was always so cold at Ma and Pa's too, even when I was a girl. You remember the winter when I was sixteen and the snow and rain would not let up until April that year."

"Ah darlin', it wasn't this cold in Ireland ever. But since I came to Iowa, I've been cold. Why just last week when we were painting the hallways of Mrs. McGreery's house, she had a fancy thermometer outside and we saw it measured at 2 degrees below freezing! And with that north wind blowin'. I would like to live where it's not so dreary in the town all day, just black and gray, day in day out. And the girls, Mary and Margaret, they sure could benefit from outdoor play in the streets in the winter with Richard's little ones. I would love to walk outside in the wintertime as free as a bird. What do you say, love? Is it time right now that we set sail?"

"Oh, Patrick, I say, yes! We could take my sister Kate with us to help take care of the girls, and with the long voyage. I have heard that it's wild out there in the West, though. How would we go?"

"We'd have to take Richard's advice. Why, we would have to sail down the Mississippi and around the Horn of South America. Anna, I think now that Vicksburg's open we can take the chance of going down the Mississippi in safety. I hear from the riverboat captains in town that the river's still open and the Union side is still prevailing. I'm weary of the war, the cold, and staying inside half the year. Richard can help me get work. We have money saved. In spite of it all, I still feel young, my darling. At 44, I'll be the youngest oldest worker on those San Francisco scaffoldings!"

"It's been decided then, Pat. We'll go off to California this spring. Off to California to the sunshine, and let's just hope that your brother is not too big of a storyteller. Why, I just cannot imagine it—what will I ever do with all my winter coats out West, with it bein' 70 degrees in February? Imagine that, imagine that, Patrick Francis Anson, imagine that!"

The Civil War would rage on for nearly another year and a half. But Anna and Patrick began to plan their voyage around the Horn in earnest, to meet up with his brother Richard's family and make a new life in San Francisco. Even if it meant a three-month-long trip sailing to San Francisco from Iowa, they would take the chance. After all, Patrick had sailed all the way from Ireland almost twenty years before. This time as well, he would put his faith in God and pray that once again taking to the seas to endure another ocean voyage would bring good fortune for him and his family. As for Anna, her home state of Iowa had seen too much heartache for her. Both her parents were gone now. There was not much to hold her to Muscatine but memories of hard times. Her middle sister, Ellen, had already married, and she planned to bring her youngest sister Kate with her.

And with that, my great-great-grandparents Patrick Francis Anson and Anna Marie McCrow Anson set off for California in the spring of 1864. He was forty-four, Anna was twenty-four. They traveled with their two daughters: Marie Louise, who was almost five, and Margaret (they called her Etta), who was just two years old. Anna's sister Kate was sixteen that spring as she set off to make the journey with them. Patrick's mother Margaret Anson was settled with his brother Michael and his wife in Muscatine. It must have been difficult for Patrick and Anna to leave her, but we can imagine that, now that Patrick had been spared in the war, Margaret wished them Godspeed on their journey to join his brother Richard and make a new life in a golden city of the West.

San Francisco, "Bird's-eye view," lithograph by Charles Gifford, 1862 (Library of Congress)

Patrick, Anna and the family arrived in San Francisco that summer, after a long voyage, and moved in with Patrick's brother Richard and his family. Richard owned a grocery and liquor store in the city on the corner of Geary and Larkin. The home address appears to be 909 Geary. They lived with Richard's family a year or two, then moved to a rental on Myrtle Street, between Larkin & Polk, according to listings in San Francisco City Directories of the time. Patrick's brother Richard was also a house painter and was listed as such in the San Francisco City Directory, as with his grocery and liquor business. The two brothers often took painting jobs together. It didn't take long for the family to settle into their bustling and entertaining new town.

Patrick Anson & Anna McCrow Anson, circa 1870s (Private Collection, Nancy Basque)

Anna and Patrick and a Former Acquaintance
~San Francisco, October 1866~

"Look here, Patrick," Anna said to Patrick one evening. "That fellow we knew in Muscatine, the riverboat captain on the Mississippi, is speaking on Tuesday at McGuire's Academy of Music. You remember him, I think—Sam Clemens. Now he's calling himself Mark Twain."

"Ahh, yes. I remember," Patrick said. "A bit of a character back in Iowa, that one, always something to say. Mark Twain, well that's a new moniker to me. What's he going to talk about, now?"

"He's going to lecture on the Sandwich Islands in Hawaii. Oh, dear, let's go. The Music Hall is only ten blocks from here, on Pine near Montgomery. We can walk there. The Dress Circle seats are $1, but the Family Circle tickets are 50¢ each. I have a dollar saved, Pat. Let's go and hear what he's got to say. It will be fun. See here, the advertisement's humorous."

Patrick sighed inwardly, but didn't let it show. *Here we go again,* he thought. *She's bringin' me to some quack show, and I may be sittin' and sufferin' through it.* As usual, he would never deny what he called a "cultural" request of Anna's, be it the theater or a lecture. This new town of San Francisco had plenty to offer in the way of entertainment. He glanced at the announcement in the Amusements column of that day's paper, which began "The Trouble Starts At Eight." He had to admit the fellow did have a knack for humor.

"All right, Anna," he said, "we'll get Richard and Mary to watch the girls. I'll get cleaned up from my job early. You know, there's still fine weather in this town, even now in October, so I was going to work late into the evenings this week finishing up the eaves of that new painting job. But I'll make an exception for Tuesday night, my dear."

"Splendid, splendid," Anna replied.

Anna walked the mile to McGuire's that morning on her way to the grocery. She stopped to admire the new hats in the Schmitt and Steiner hat shop on Market Street. "Look at this one, girls," she said as she lifted her young daughters up to the window. Both girls gazed wide-eyed at the newest fashions, fancy ribbons surrounding crepe de chine bonnets. "Someday, someday," she hoped, "we'll be able to buy you these lovely things too."

The Trouble Starts at Eight

From DAILY ALTA CALIFORNIA,

Advertisement, *San Francisco Call Bulletin,* October 2, 1865

Downtown San Francisco, Occidental Hotel, Montgomery St, 1860s (Library of Congress)

It turned out that the tickets for the evening with Mr. Twain were just about sold out, but Anna bought two tickets. *He'll enjoy this lecture*, she mused, *I just know it. I think even better than he knows. Why, Patrick met Sam Clemens in Muscatine plenty of times, while picking up paint cans and windows shipped from St Louis. I think he'll remember his gay repartee as the lecture goes on.* She headed home back to 909 Geary. While Anna cooked dinner that night, her daughters played tiddlywinks in the parlor.

Pat's brother Richard arrived home to the upstairs flat and popped his head in to shout "Halloo." Richard's brogue was even a bit thicker than Pat's. Anna would tease the both of them. "You sound like you're back in Ireland," she'd smile, but in fact their lilting Irish speech reminded her fondly of both her parents. She remembered each one had lullabied her to sleep many nights with their lovely Irish tongues, singing "Too Ra Loo Ra Loo Ral." Neither she nor her daughters had inherited the brogue, as they were all American born.

Patrick headed home that light-filled late summer night and arrived by 7 pm, hungry and tired. "Did you get the tickets to Mr. Sam Clemens' lecture?" he asked.

"Yes, barely. It will be sold out, so be home by 5:30 tomorrow, Pat. I'll wash your shirt and tie. Your coat's clean. It's time we go out more on this town. You remember the lectures we went to in Muscatine, dear? Now, lectures here in San Francisco are so much more entertaining."

Patrick spent the next day preparing the house on Van Ness for its first coat of color. He and his brother, who had taken a few days away from his grocery store for this paint job, had primed and whitewashed the newly built three-story house last week. They had a good sense of color, helping the lady of the house pick out the main colors and trim. But neither Anson brothers were looking forward to painting the elaborate trim, with all the "gingerbread" those architects down on Montgomery Street had drawn up. There were turrets and curved beams running around the rooftop gutters. Not one gargoyle, though, Patrick thought and he was glad of that; he'd seen enough of that downtown. As painting jobs, though, he couldn't complain. This one was a large house and got him outside for most of the day. With the warm afternoon sun on his back, Patrick still felt satisfied about their decision to move out West.

"The last winters in Iowa were just about as cold as I ever remembered bein'," he shouted to Richard as they stood high on the scaffold, their brushes finishing up the last high beam. The view of the new city from their perch was magnificent in the warm October sun. San Francisco Bay was gleaming, its blue water reflecting the cloudless Indian summer sky.

"Now you know I wasn't tellin' you no stories," Richard shouted back. "This is a golden city. I knew it right away as soon as I stepped off the boat six years ago. And I felt in my bones that you, Anna, and the girls would fit right in. What with all the sleet, snow and gray days in Iowa, it was even colder than our dear old Ireland, right Pat?"

"Ah, yer right. I don't miss Iowa so much, but I sometimes long to see Ma back in Muscatine. I know she gets our letters, but 'tis a shame she can't see our faces. The San Francisco fog is a bit of a consolation to me, as it reminds me of the old sod. Anna likes it well enough here. She's beginning to write her articles again for the literary journals."

"That so?" asked Richard.

"Well you know how smart she is, always has a point of view, that's for sure. When I married her, I knew I had a gem. She's wantin' us to go to see Mark Twain tonight. You remember him from Muscatine, eh?"

Richard thought a moment between brush strokes. "Yeah, Pat, I do. He's the riverboat captain, Sam Clemens, who's taken that new name. Had his start at his brother's print shop up the street from us there on Third and Bryant along the Mississippi. Clever gentleman, right. I used to see him when I purchased the fancy St. Louis paint at the Muscatine docks."

"Yeah, that's him all right. He's been writing for the *Alta California*, and the *Call Bulletin* here in the City. 'Course Anna reads all those papers she can get her hands on. The lecture's sold out."

Pat checked his pocket watch. "It's half past four. I've got to be home early, get all dressed up and out of these paintin' clothes. See you tomorrow at 8 am sharp."

Patrick climbed down the scaffolding easily. At age 45, he was fit and trim. Both brothers had been housepainters most of their adult lives, with Richard also running his grocery and liquor store. They put together a living. They had tried roofing as well back in Iowa, but decided to stick to painting. Sometimes Richard introduced his big brother Pat as "Captain Anson" in respect of his time in the Civil War. Both brothers loved living near the San Francisco Bay, with its cool nights and warm summer days.

Mark Twain, 1867 (Library of Congress)

Mark Twain was quite entertaining that night. Patrick had to hand it to him, he did have a great gift for telling tales. The lecture lasted an hour and a half, and the sold-out crowd gave him the applause he deserved. Patrick concluded that Anna and her literary ideas were pretty good after all.

That evening in San Francisco was the first of Mark Twain's lifetime of humorous and informative public lectures. The 1860s were long before the days of a radio in every home. For evening entertainment, folks read, sewed, sang songs or played music. And they went out to lectures, theater, opera or music concerts.

Mark Twain lived in San Francisco for only two years. He had mixed success as a local reporter, and never returned to the City. Apparently, he never said the famous line: "The coldest winter I ever spent was summer in San Francisco." But San Francisco was the very first place where Mark Twain walked onto a stage. The topic of his lecture was Hawaii—then known as the Sandwich Islands—where he had spent nearly half a year. For that first lecture, which today we would call stand-up comedy, he made up a poster with these words: "Doors Open at 7 1/2, The Trouble Starts at Eight." It was the beginning of a lifelong success for Mark Twain as a performer.

The San Francisco Bay Area turned out to be the incubator for the next waves of entertainment. In 1872, the rich industrialist Leland Stanford invited San Francisco photographer Eadweard Muybridge to his Palo Alto farm to photograph a horse in motion, which began the important technology of motion pictures, or "the movies." Later in 1878, Mr. Muybridge set up and showed the first moving picture in Stanford's San Francisco mansion on Nob Hill. It would be forty years before silent movies were shown in neighborhood theaters, which would play an im-

"Horses Running", Eadweard Muybridge, photographer, Palo Alto CA, circa 1881 (Library of Congress)

portant role in Patrick and Anna's granddaughter Lottie's adult life. As for home entertainment, radio broadcasts began thirty years later in the dawn of the new century of the 1900s. Television had yet to be thought of, much less invented, until Philo T. Farnsworth, one of TV's first inventors, began tinkering with vacuum tubes in his San Francisco laboratory at 220 Green Street in 1927. You may be reading this on the computer, which has its birthplace in Palo Alto in the San Francisco Bay area, just around the corner from where I grew up.

CHAPTER 4
Coming of Age in San Francisco
1864-1885

I have heard about my great-grandmother Marie Louise for years—Patrick and Anna's oldest child, born in Muscatine, Iowa. All the stories about Marie Louise came from my mother, her granddaughter. My mother didn't remember Marie Louise alive, but she did remember her funeral, when my mother was only three. Marie Louise had shared her stories with her daughter, my grandmother Charlotte, who told them to my mother. My mother told these stories to me, about Marie Louise's life in San Francisco and on the Sacramento Delta. Through these stories, and today realizing that my mother gave me her grandmother's name Marie as my middle name, I feel close to Marie Louise. I see that I have come to know her. I know her story. Like me, she married twice, got divorced once, was a single mother for a while, and found happiness in her long second marriage.

When I visited her gravesite, her tombstone simply said Marie Louise Smith. I finally found her in Holy Cross Cemetery in Colma, just south of San Francisco. I laid down next to her, the wind whistled above and all around, and her voice, her kindness, her stature came through easily, as awakenings often do.

Marie Louise Anson Smith
~1864~

I was born in the spring of 1859 in Muscatine, Iowa to my parents Anna and Patrick Anson, just as the snow was beginning to melt. It was cold, cold, freezing in Iowa. My mother had to dress me in woolens from early fall all the way past my April 22 birthday. Then when my sister Margaret came along, there were two to wrap up against the winter chill. Even though my mother was born and raised in Iowa, she told my father that it was too hard on us girls to live out our lives in that frozen climate. She wanted more for her family. She wanted to feel warm in the sunshine, and if she could live by the ocean (she'd never been, of course) that would be heavenly.

So, when my father received letters from his brother Richard in San Francisco, telling how the weather in winter was 70 degrees, that was enticing enough to get my parents to make the long sail out West. We up and moved in 1864. We sailed down the Mississippi, boarded a ship bound for California that April, and landed at the San Francisco docks that summer. When we stepped off the ship, Uncle Richard was waiting for us. He had hired two horse carriages to carry my parents, myself, my sister Etta and my aunt Kate with our trunks on Market Street's wide cobblestones, up Montgomery, past Chinatown, and on to his residence near the southwest corner of Geary and Larkin streets.

Market Street, San Francisco, circa 1860s
(Library of Congress)

My first ride on the streets of San Francisco, California brought me face to face with sights that I as a young five-year-old had never seen! There were Chinese workers with their long pigtails, horse-drawn street cars clanging their bells up and down the hills, and big buildings—even six-story buildings along Market Street that were marvelous to me! After that long, almost three-month sail round Cape Horn in South America, you can bet I was glad to see dry land and fantastic city.

My mother and father said San Francisco was the most lively and exciting place they had ever seen. I guess that's why they settled here and rented a house so near the whole Anson family, with a bay window so we could look out on the downtown and see a glimpse of the Bay towards the east, where the sun came up. If you rode up the big hill, you could see what everyone calls the Golden Gate, the passageway for all the ships. Over the next years my sisters Cecelia and Amy were born at home in the City, along with

Horse-drawn streetcar, downtown San Francisco, circa 1860 (SF Municipal Transportation Agency)

my brothers Joe, Paul and Arthur. My parents quickly learned to hop on the horse-drawn City Municipal streetcars to tour over the hills of the City. We rode downtown on Sundays to see the finery in the windows of the new City of Paris department store.

Our small family travelled by horse and buggy way out to the Cliff House by the beach. I must tell you that the bathing suits we girls had to wear were woolen, scratchy and itchy, but it was worth it to me to dip into the Pacific Ocean on the rare warm days we would have in September and October. The City in truth was actually colder than we were led to believe, but it was never as cold as Iowa! Many days the wind whipped through the streets of San Francisco, swirling dust into our clothes and hats. Still, we got used to the fog and

San Francisco Cliff House, 1860 (Library of Congress)

chilly nights of the summer. We did have a few surprise earthquakes that year of our arrival in 1864. Our chandelier shook and swayed back and forth. My mother grabbed my hand and rushed outside, crying, "Lord save us all!"

I grew up happy and content in San Francisco, as I felt we were here to stay. I went to the Notre Dame Girls' School all the way through high school, where I got good marks. After high school, I worked at home helping mother and father. I sewed clothes for all our family: pinafores, warm coats for winter, dresses for friends' weddings and such. When I was twenty-one, I was able to work as a professional dressmaker. Then it was my time to get married, and at almost twenty-two years I felt ready to have my own home and begin to have children.

I was married to Benjamin Garrett in St Brigid's Church in San Francisco on February 22, 1881. Our daughter Charlotte was born three years later, in 1884. My mother thought Mr. Garrett was a good catch because he was well to do, but all I caught from him was a broken heart. How was I to know he had another wife!

What you heard about my first marriage is correct. My first husband, Mr. Benjamin Garrett, was indeed a bigamist. My divorce is there in the records. The *San Francisco Chronicle* on January 1, 1885, published it in black and white for the whole town to see. Under the heading of "Mismatched Couples," my name stands in shame and embarrassment: "*Garrett-Mary L. from John B. December 4; extreme cruelty.*" Yes, my name was right there, one of those 391 divorces in San Francisco in that year. Oh, that scoundrel! I was married less than three years, with my new baby Charlotte in my arms! What could I do but become divorced, go back to 610 Larkin and live with my parents in shame? Some people would refer to my family as "broken," but I rankled against that word. I thought, *My family is not broken, it's just different.* I loved my daughter Charlotte no less than any other mother did. In any case, I was glad to say good riddance to Mr. Benjamin Garrett. He never did help with Charlotte's finances, not one dime all through her childhood.

When the divorce was finalized, I realized that I had my beautiful daughter, Charlotte, who I called Lottie, and I gathered my wits about me. I had to work to make a living, and by God, that's just what I did. From the time I was a little girl, I loved clothes, loved the way they look on a person. Finely tailored dresses and handsomely cut suits were a joy for me to make and to see others wear. I had to support both Lottie and myself, so I began to take on clients who saw my work displayed in the seamstress shop on Sansome Street, where I was paid as a dressmaker. Those days, I made many fine wedding dresses and fancy evening clothes for women. It was my joy to sew, both by the treadle machine and by doing handwork, beading, lace and embroidery. It was this that led me to the final and best chapters of my life.

PART TWO
The Sacramento Delta

1886–1902

---- CHAPTER 5 ----
Up the Sacramento River
1886-1894

M arie Louise's first daughter, my grandmother Charlotte (Lottie) Smith, was born in San Francisco, but she grew up playing in the farmlands of the Sacramento Delta. Lottie had a full and free childhood there, was crowned May Queen when she was eleven years old, and attended an excellent Catholic boarding school where she received a refined European education. The fact that life brought Marie Louise and her young daughter Lottie to the Delta meant a good turn of fate for all.

Marie Louise Anson Smith
~1886~

It was several months after my divorce that Mrs. Maggie Smith commissioned my mother and I to sew some dress clothes and everyday wear for her large family of ten children, herself and her husband, in the town of Isleton in the Sacramento Delta. Mrs. Smith had seen my fine clothes on display in the City and asked if we would be able to make the sailing trip upriver to take measurements of her large brood. She explained that she felt there was no one in the small nearby Delta towns of Rio Vista, Isleton, Ryde or Walnut Grove to match our dressmaking skills.

Mother and I both were happy to oblige. Mrs. Smith made the arrangements and paid our tickets on the steamship and the transfer on the sloop. The next week we boarded the ship to sail from San Francisco Bay up the Sacramento River to Isleton with our sewing things: needles, pins, rulers, hem guide, scissors,

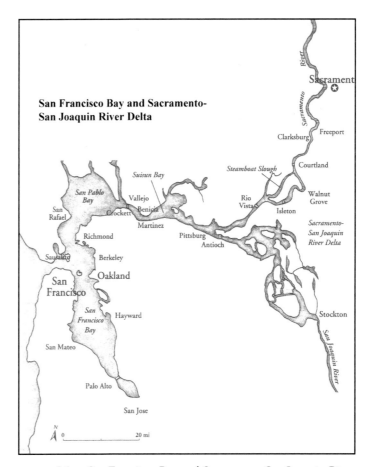

Map, San Francisco Bay and Sacramento-San Joaquin River Delta. Marie Louise visited Garrett Smith traveling east by boat from San Francisco to Isleton (Stan Garvey, *King and Queen of the River*, 2008)

and a small valise of fabric samples. Of course, we would take the measurements there and return to the City to sew all of the family's clothes, which we would pack up to return again for the final fittings. The trip was overnight on the steamship, leaving San Francisco at 5 pm from the Ferry Building and arriving on the landing dock of the Smith home at 5 am the next morning. We were happy for this commission, as it secured our fortunes for the next while. Little did I know I would get a husband out of the bargain as well, but that is indeed what happened.

Garrett Smith, the eldest son of the Smith family, was twenty-two at our first encounter in Isleton. I was twenty-six. By then, he had a working farm and owned 60 acres of pears and asparagus on Grand Island. Garrett's father Hart F. Smith had given him this property as an inheritance. Hart Smith's original properties were 595 acres, which he purchased from the United States government after the California Land Act of 1851. These acres had been originally tule/marsh lands, and Garrett's father, along with hired Chinese laborers, had built low levees using wheelbarrows and shovels in the 1860s. I heard that the Delta lands were originally filled with mosquitoes, and back in those days had many more natural islands. When I arrived, there were so many levees that helped hold the water away from the farmlands. The farmers were trying to conquer the natural flow of the waters from the Sierra Mountains that drained through the Delta into the San Francisco Bay. These levees, as I would come to find out when I resided there, broke during high water years and at times flooded our ranch. You see, in reality all of the farmlands stood below sea level, and the dikes kept the natural flow of the water from them.

But I am getting ahead of myself. From our first meeting, Garrett Smith was so kind to me. I myself knew he was a good prospect. He courted me long distance. I was living in San Francisco, and he had the ranch to look after, 56 miles up the Sacramento River. It was so romantic and yet difficult to have a long-distance love affair.

Garrett would sail in to San Francisco on a schooner loaded with his farm's bounty of peaches, pears, asparagus, wheat, barley and melons. After landing on the dock by the old Ferry Building, he'd board the cable car up Market Street to knock on our door, bearing crates of vegetables and fruit picked just the day before. Oh, we did enjoy the pears especially! The sweet last taste of summer lasted all year, as we canned many in glass jars for the winter.

River steamers at San Francisco Wharf, by Lawrence and Houseworth, late 1800s (Library of Congress)

I loved to sail up to the Delta country to visit the Smiths' ranch. It was a joy to me to see such wide-open country as we passed by the hills of the East Bay, Benicia, through the Carquinez Straits and into the Delta itself. I could always tell the seasons by the songs and sights of the birds who flew in and out of this marshy land: thousands upon thousands of egrets, blue herons, pelicans, snow geese, and so many types of ducks! Flocks upon flocks of mallards and cinnamon teals flew overhead; sometimes they blackened the skies! The flapping of their wings and the cry of their songs was an overpowering sight to see.

To my surprise, even after my divorce and having a young daughter, Garrett Smith proposed marriage to me. My mother knew that I had chosen well, and when Garrett and I were engaged, I was over the moon at the prospect of our lives together. My then two-year-old daughter Lottie loved him too, and he was so good to her. I could tell he would be an excellent father and provider. Garrett and I made plans for the wedding, which was held in San Francisco on February 1, 1886. He officially adopted Lottie in 1898 and was a true father to her. I made my lovely wedding dress when I married Garrett Smith.

Now, please, please do try to get this straight—just because my first husband was Benjamin Garrett, and my second steadfast, true, loyal husband was Garrett Smith, try to keep

Marie Louise Anson and Garrett Smith, wedding day, Feb. 1, 1886 (Private Collection, Nancy Basque

them in your mind as two different men. Grandpa Smith was kind and generous. Benjamin Garrett only gave me pain. I will never forgive one of Lottie's classmates for telling her the gossip at St Gertrude's boarding school, that she was a bastard child. In the first place, she wasn't a bastard child at all. I was legally married to my first husband when Lottie was born. Of course, Lottie wanted to know the truth about him, ever since that day in the fall of 1898 when she heard the gossip. We just didn't talk about those things then. Poor girl, she was only fourteen years old, such a vulnerable age. When she asked, I told her, "Yes, darling, your father is Benjamin Garrett. He lives in San Francisco now."

Over Lottie's next three years, curiosity got the best of her, and she arranged to meet Benjamin Garret in San Francisco. He gave her $500 and a brooch, and it must have meant something to her, for it was the one she wore on her wedding dress. Lottie and I didn't talk much about Mr. Benjamin Garrett after that. I still felt ashamed to have seen my name in the newspapers and sad that such a scandal had blemished my life. The record of my first husband Benjamin Garrett's death in the Agnew State Hospital in San Jose is true. It turned out that scoundrel had all along been married to a woman named Charlotte—the name of his firstborn daughter, my Charlotte. Now that is beyond me!

It's funny how the hard knocks of life can push you around. Yet in those times of turmoil, it seems like fate can send you into the arms of the right one. Just after you felt like there may not be a true love in your life, the one appears, and everything's just right from then on. We had three more children together: Veda, Warren and Hart. Of course, Lottie was two years old when we married, so she was a natural part of the brood. Later, my mother Anna and my father Patrick, who was still called "Captain Anson," came to live in the Delta. It was the fulfilment of all I could wish for.

Wedding photo of Marie Louise and Garrett Smith, standing at right. Bottom left are her parents, Anna and Patrick Anson (Private Collection, Nancy Basque)

CHAPTER 6
The Delta
1886-1894

Life was busy on the ranch. Marie Louise was raising four children, cooking, and managing the house. Garrett tended their pear orchards and oversaw the farm's sales, packaging and shipping fruit and vegetables throughout the Bay Area. Isleton was such a busy agricultural area that it was known as the "Asparagus Capital of the World." Marie Louise likely enjoyed sewing all the clothing for their family and for some of her husband's siblings' families. Marie Louise's parents, Anna and Patrick joined her in the Delta, and lived much of the rest of their lives there. Much older now, Anna reminded Marie Louise that Muscatine, where they'd

Vegetable crate label showing Sacramento River
(Author Collection)

44

both been born, was known as the "Pearl of the Mississippi" for its buttons made from the mussel shells harvested from the river. Marie Louise never forgot her birthplace each time she carefully sewed buttons on her own clothes.

Over the years, Garrett and Marie Louise had a full social life in Isleton. They loved to attend grand parties at Garrett's brother Hart's four-story house, which many referred to as a mansion. The food was elegant, and Hart had butlers and cut-glass chandeliers hanging from the high ceilings. It amused Marie Louse, the way Hart wore a fez on his head with his smoking jacket, as the men retired to the den after dinner to play poker, while the women played more genteel games in the parlor.

Drawing of Hart F. Smith's ranch (brother of Garrett Smith) near Sacramento Delta (Smith Family Collection.)

All the family loved watching Garrett's youngest brother, Warren (Locomotive) Smith's achievements in sports. At UC Berkeley, he earned varsity letters in three sports: football, baseball and track and field. At one point, Warren was regarded as the top college halfback on the West Coast. He led the Berkeley Golden Bears to their first two football victories over Stanford in 1898 and 1899. He was the captain of Berkeley's football *and* baseball teams, and scored points for track and field in the hammer throw as well. Warren was the first player ever to score three touchdowns in the big game of UC Berkeley versus Stanford. Garrett attended many games to see his little brother outrun the competition.

Marie Louise joined the Catholic church group, the Daughters of Isabella, in Isleton and there found many friends and a way to help others in need through the group's charitable acts. She was devoted to her children Charlotte, Veda, Warren and Hart Francis, and was glad to provide them all with good educations through the Catholic schools in Isleton.

Their oldest daughter Lottie lived full time on the ranch in the Sacramento Delta for several years. When she was eight years old, Marie Louise decided to send Lottie to St. Gertrude's Academy for Girls in Rio Vista, a boarding school five miles downriver from home.

The story of my great-grandfather Garrett Smith's pocket watch was told to me by my mother's brother Uncle Phil Lynch, as he was driving on the Sacramento Delta levees in 1992. Uncle Phil was an excellent storyteller, a salesman by trade. While driving my mother, myself and my two daughters along the Delta levees, he loved to tell anecdotes about our people who came before, how they lived, and what their times were like on the Delta rivers when he and his parents lived there. This story takes place in the winter of 1892.

Garrett Smith and The Pocket Watch

Sacramento River, Isleton
~Saturday, December 19, 1892~

Garrett Smith knew he still had two miles to row until he would arrive at St. Gertrude's Academy at the Rio Vista dock. He was barely able to gauge the distance to the upcoming bridge, although he'd passed these curves all his life. The wind was pushing the rain sideways now, and he wished he'd asked his brother Hart to row with him. But there was no way that Garrett could have known at the beginning of this trip how bad the storm would become, otherwise he would have taken the extra half hour to tie his boat to Hart's landing, walk up the pier, and slosh into the house to see if his brother would accompany him on his row to pick up Lottie for Christmas vacation.

Garrett didn't even ask one of the farmworkers from the Chong family to help, although he felt they would have, given the fact that all the Chinese laborers worked so hard on the ranch. Why, they had built the levees that made his farm possible. And Lottie, his first daughter, was the apple of everyone's eye. He sensed that everyone on the ranch was affected too, when his oldest daughter was sent downriver to Saint Gertrude's as a boarder last September. Lottie had played often with all the children on the ranch over the years, but friendship between a white girl and Chinese children was not proper according to Lottie's mother, Marie Louise.

As he rowed into the storm, Garrett thought how he'd grown up right here in Isleton and gone to school here too. He knew that the Chinese had their own separate school. When he was a young boy, in his eyes they all seemed to get along. Now that he managed the ranch, he knew the facts—there were many cultures in the Delta. Farms like his depended on hardworking Chinese, Japanese and Filipino peoples. And now his first daughter was sent away downriver to boarding school. He sort of saw the sense in sending Lottie to the finest school, where she could get, as Marie Louise said, a "European education." Yet Garrett missed his little daughter's daily spark of laughter and the brightness she brought to all of them. It was worth it to him to row on and bring her back home for the holidays.

The wind was pushing the rain sideways now, and once again he wished he'd asked his brother Hart to row with him two hours ago. But there was no way that Garrett could have known at the beginning of this trip how bad the storm would become.

The wind was howling past his freezing hands. "Damn this river," he cried to no one at all. The wind answered him with another strong gust. Cursing out loud to the Sacramento River was something he never had heard himself do before this day, although he'd heard his dad and his friends curse the river and the power it had to knock down the levees like children's playthings in its path. Garrett's family told stories of the winters of 1864–66, when they had seen massive floods all over the newly claimed Delta. Most all the new farms were wiped out completely. White landowners had hired Chinese workers to build the levees several times over since then, each time stronger, or so they hoped.

"I hope this storm calms soon." Garrett prayed and rowed, prayed and rowed, as he looked skyward.

Chinese laborers build levees on Sacramento Delta
(*Overland Monthly*, 1896)

At St. Gertrude's Academy, young Lottie watched out the window at the fierce storm. "Sister Camillus, how much longer?" she whined.

"Oh, just a few more minutes," Camillus answered, looking out of the west-facing window again, searching for any sign of Garrett Smith. The rain was beating on the old panes of glass. *I hope the caulk holds against this wind*, she prayed, while she fingered her rosary beads and looked skyward.

"Finish your lunch and we'll play tiddlywinks in the downstairs parlor. I will help you with your suitcase for the trip. I think you'd better wear this extra mackintosh over your own. Did we pack two sets of galoshes?"

"No, Sister. Why, I don't have two pairs, Mama only sent me with the one. You remember the list, don't you, Sister? Gosh, that wind's making too much noise. I can hardly see out the window for the rain! Look, there's a little water coming in the dormitory window by Laura Orth's bed!"

"Oh well, Lottie, I'll put a towel there, not to worry," she told the young girl. Sister Camillus began to worry about the windows again. But with nothing to be done right away, she fingered her rosary again.

St. Gertrude's Academy, Rio Vista, circa 1890s (Rio Vista Museum)

Just then a loud knock sounded on the front door, over the howling wind. "Oh Lottie, that must by your Papa," Camillus said hopefully.

"Hooray!" shouted Lottie as she raced down the stairs, flung open the door and hugged Garrett tighter than he'd remembered she could.

"Oh, my darling girl, you've grown!" He returned her hug with equal measure.

"Papa, you're all wet! Did you come alone? Is Uncle Hart with you?"

"No, Lottie, just me. Now let's get your things."

Camillus interrupted at that moment, insisting that he must stay and sit by the parlor fireplace to at least thaw out and dry off somewhat before their return trip back to Isleton. "I feel the storm's abating a bit, Mr. Smith. It will be better for you both to sit."

Sister Camillus, Mother Superior, St. Gertrude's Academy, circa 1880s (Rio Vista Museum)

She served him hot tea and cookies that were left over from the Christmas festivities at St. Gertrude's two nights ago, before school let out.

"I am sorry, Sister, that I had to pick up our girl so late this time, but what with yesterday's inundation, I had to wait for what I thought was a bit of a clearing this morning. You know, when I left the wind hadn't picked up, until about fifteen minutes into the row. I know these rivers, Sister, but I've never seen it so fierce out there as this morning."

"Look at it now, look out at the hills, Papa! There's blue sky over there above Mt. Diablo, I see it! Let's go!"

Garrett stood, remembering the long row ahead. "All right, Miss Lottie, we'll be on our way. Button up your mackintosh and galoshes. My overcoat's a bit dry now. Let's check the time and see how fast we'll get back home now; after all, the current is against us on the way home. Mama's all ready for you, got her tea set all laid out."

He took his gold pocket watch out of his vest. Small beads of moisture had begun to form on the face of his trusted timepiece. "Well see, Lottie, it's quarter past one. We'll be along, now. No need to help with the valise, Sister, I've got it. Lottie, take your muff, you'll need it. Thanks so much, Sister, for waiting with our girl."

"No need to thank me, Mr. Smith. Now I will say a prayer for both of you, home safe and sound, safe and sound. Godspeed," Camillus said as she waved.

"Thanks again."

"Thank you, Sister," called Lottie, waving back.

They headed for the dock where the small rowboat bobbed in the water. The water was calmer, without the tall waves it had held earlier that morning.

Lottie stepped into the rowboat first. "Papa, we're going to have to bail some of this out. It's a little wet."

Indeed, the rain had filled the rowboat with about an inch of water. "Let's get to it, girl." He handed her the small bucket and he took the other and they began a familiar routine, bailing first, as they'd had

Sacramento River, 1871 (Hutchings, *Scenes of Wonder and Curiosity in California*, reprint 2010)

to do over the years, then checking and setting the oars. He told her he'd row first and maybe the whole trip, depending on the weather. Even though he was tired, he knew his eight-year-old daughter didn't yet know the current, and wasn't strong enough nor an expert in the ways of wind and water like he was.

They began. By now the storm had abated enough so they could converse a bit; only a few raindrops slashed the rowboat.

"How is the school? Your marks are so high, Lottie. Do you like the teachers, I mean the sisters?" He hadn't had any experience with nuns, or sisters as the Catholics called them. To Garrett they seemed like a friendly lot, but he couldn't understand why they never married. He was so happy being married to Marie Louise that he was flummoxed as to why a whole group of women would say no to the notion of marriage. But Garrett knew that Marie Louise had had a very good education in the Catholic Notre Dame School in the City. His wife knew about fancy things that he never had learned in the Isleton Grammar School, things like painting, elocution, European writing, like that. He hoped this venture of sending Lottie to boarding school would be the right thing for his bright daughter. He rowed on.

"Papa, the sisters are nice to me. I like Sister Camillus. She's a good teacher, but there are some that are too strict. You have to go to bed too early and get up sometimes when you're not ready. The older girls are nice to us, but there's one girl in my grade who's mean. She says that I am too skinny and my hair's too red, and my curls are not combed right. I wanted to hit her, but Sister Camillus says I can't. When she's mean like that, I miss my friends back at the ranch."

Classroom, St. Gertrude's Academy, circa 1890s (Rio Vista Museum)

Garrett listened contentedly to Lottie's stories as he rowed. The trip home was much quicker. They arrived on their dock in scattered rain and instantly were greeted by the arms of their family, as Marie Louise came rushing out to swoop up Lottie into her arms.

"Let's get the both of you dry, Garrett," said Marie Louise. "I was worried sick about you both in this terrible storm."

"Well, I'll get dry, change my clothes and meet you for dinner," Garrett replied.

He took a hot bath upstairs that late afternoon. As he took off his soaked vest, he checked his pocket watch, musing that it had been many hours since he began his solo journey upriver that early morning. So much rain had seeped in that the watch face was beaded inside with drops. The watch, which his father Hart had given him when he was eighteen, had stopped at exactly 2:14 pm. It never ran right again. Since that stormy day, Garrett would try at different times to get his favorite watch to correct itself, but it always held that bit of moisture to remind him of that rainy trip on the Sacramento on Saturday, December 19, 1892.

Garrett Smith, 1920, Lottie's stepfather
(Author Collection)

GARRETT D. SMITH
AGRICULTURIST
BOX 13, R. F. D., No. 1
WALNUT GROVE, CALIFORNIA

Garrett Smith letterhead
(Author Collection)

CHAPTER 7
May Queen
1895

One spring afternoon in 1959, when I was nine years old, I slid the doors of my mother's back closet open to discover a treasure trove of old scrapbooks, fading newspapers, and black-and-white photos of my grandparents. I pulled out my grandmother Charlotte's brown scrapbook with the Scottie dog embossed on it, laid it down on the hall floor, and thumbed through.

It was a quiet afternoon, and my mother felt that I could stay home by myself in the daytime. My brother Pat was most likely playing baseball for his high school team, and my sister Sue was probably somewhere with her high school friends. We had a modern ranch-style 1950s house in Palo Alto, rambling with four bedrooms, two large hall closets, and a big backyard. I already knew what was in the bedrooms and I knew every inch of the backyard by then, but the hall closets were left to be explored

To me, the newspaper articles in this scrapbook were incredibly old. I could tell because the paper was frayed, and the typeface was so different than the *San Francisco Chronicle* that

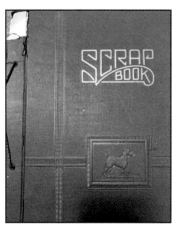

Charlotte Smith Lynch's scrapbook (Author Collection)

arrived on our doorstep every morning. The article below is the oldest one pasted in the scrapbook. It describes the day when my grandmother Lottie was appointed May Queen of the Delta Islands at eleven years old.

I have read and reread this lovely article many times over the years. Please read it carefully and slowly. (The original article is followed by an easier-to-read version.) Imagine Lottie's proud mother, Marie Louise, clipping the article carefully while she fondly remembered this day in May when her 11-year-old daughter was May Queen. Imagine her grandparents Anna Anson and Captain Anson, now living on the Delta, who were part of this day. Anna Anson, known as a literary woman who contributed articles to local press and magazines, may very well have been the "Witness" who penned the article. Notice the mention of Captain Anson—that is Lottie's grandfather Patrick, who fought in the Civil War. Imagine the bower, the boat sailing up the Sacramento River decorated

Picnic of St. Gertrude's Academy.

On Thursday, May 2, the pupils of St. Gertrude's held their picnic at the grove of Judge H. Smith, near Vorden. The procession headed by Rev. W. D. McKinnon, the worthy pastor of Rio Vista, left the academy at 11 a. m. in the following order: The May Queen, Miss Lottie Smith, in elegant costume, with her maids of honor, Ella McGraugh and Mable Ruble, were driven in a carriage appropriately and tastefully decorated for the occasion with flowers, flags, etc.; next came the Queen's guard, consisting of about thirty school boys from the academy with Master Arthur Dunn acting as captain, under the command of Capt. Anson of Rio Vista. Then followed the May-pole children, looking bright and pretty notwithstanding the uncertainty of the weather, which prevented their being in costume. Lastly, the young ladies of the academy in whose faces, one and all, might well be read the anticipation of a day's pleasure long to be remembered. When the procession reached the wharf they boarded the Pride of Wood Island and after a delightful sail of about two hours reached the grove where the exercises were to take place. They were met there by the parents and friends of the May Queen, together with a number of the patrons of the school, who cordially welcomed them. The little May Queen and her maids were conducted to the platform in a beautiful carriage which might well be compared to a fairy bower, so beautifully was it decorated with the choicest flowers of the season. The guard filed on each side of the carriage, headed by their captain and Capt. Anson.

The program rendered was as follows:
May Queen Song......Miss Lottie Smith
Coronation................Miss May Dwyer
Presentation of Sceptre..................
..........................Miss Cleta Manley
Military Drill...............Queen's Guard
Song of Triumph.....Miss Ethel Condon
Queen's Address......Miss Lottie Smith
Braiding of May Pole....Junior Pupils

The above program was beautifully rendered, the pupils acquitting themselves in a most creditable manner of the different parts assigned to them.

The May Queen, whose noble bearing and style of delivery was wonderful in a child of 11 years, deserves special mention. Her address was as follows:

My Beloved Subjects:—

It is with pleasure that I address you on this beautiful May morning. It is many years since a Queen has been crowned by such bright, loving hands in my grandpa's beautiful grove. Perhaps not since the time of the fairies; where I am sure they must have chosen this beautiful spot to hold high revel and dance in the moonlight with their charming King and Queen; but I do not think the fairies were half so good, lovely and faithful as my dear subjects. I have taken great pains to make this a day of long-to-be-remembered pleasure for you, and I wish to see you enjoy it fully. Any favor that I am able to grant you will be a pleasure, and, my dear subjects, I will take into consideration your many needs, especially for the time when you will desire to place your ballot in the box for our new President and will require the use of the bicycle to bring you in haste to the place of meeting, for I am determined that none of my dear subjects shall be behind the times, and very lately I have heard that a young gentleman in Vallejo has invented a flying machine, and I will get one for you in order that you may visit Smith's Grove any time you desire to do so. Now be very happy today, the anticipation of all the good things provided for you, and those in store to come, should make you very happy. So one and all away and enjoy yourselves.

Capt. Anson has every reason to be proud of his well drilled soldiers, who, seeming to imbibe his spirit of enthusiasm, carried the day.

Master Arthur Dunn in full costume made a gallant little captain and acted his part in an admirable manner.

After lunch Rev. Father McKinnon in his usual genial manner returned thanks to those present for their kindness, attention, etc., and was heartily applauded.

Judge H. Smith, the owner of the grove, also, we understand, gave the free use of the grounds to the pupils of the academy and did everything to add to their comfort, all in honor of th beautiful May Queen, who is his charming little grand-daughter, and really he has reason to be proud of so bright and promising a child.

A WITNESS.

Article in *Sacramento River News,* May 10, 1895
(Charlotte's scrapbook, Author Collection)

with spring blossoms and the air soft, as you read Lottie's words to her "subjects." Put yourself in her place. The year is 1895, and she gives a speech, saying she dreams of bestowing bicycles and flying machines on each young student, on the verge of the new century to come. For most of her life, Lottie would never lose her love of performing.

Text of Article, *Sacramento River News*

FRIDAY, MAY 10, 1895

PICNIC OF ST. GERTRUDE'S ACADEMY

On Thursday, May 2, the pupils of St. Gertrude's held their picnic at the grove of Judge H. Smith near Isleton. The procession headed by Rev. W. D. McKinnon, the worthy pastor of Rio Vista, left the academy at 11 a.m. In the following order: The May Queen, Miss Lottie Smith, in elegant costume, with her maids of honor, Ella McGraugh and Mabel Ruble, were driven in a carriage appropriately and tastefully decorated for the occasion with flowers, flags, etc.; next came the Queen's Guard, consisting of about thirty school boys from the Academy, Master Arthur Dunn acting as captain, under the command of Capt. Anson of Rio Vista. Then followed the May-pole children, looking bright and pretty notwithstanding the uncertainty of the weather, which prevented their being in costume. Lastly, the young ladies of the academy in whose faces, one and all, might well be read the anticipation of a day's pleasure long to be remembered. When the procession reached the wharf they boarded the Pride of Wood Island and after a delightful sail of about two hours reached the grove where the exercises were to take place. They were met there by the parents and friends of the May Queen, together with a number of the patrons of the school, who cordially welcomed them. The little May Queen and her maids were conducted to the platform in a beautiful carriage which might well be compared to a fairy bower, so beautifully was it decorated with the choicest flowers of the season. The guard filed on each side of the carriage, headed by their captain and Capt. Anson.

The program rendered was as follows:

> May Queen Song ... Miss Lottie Smith
> Coronation ... Miss May Dwyer
> Presentation of Sceptre ... Cleta Manley
> Military Drill ... Queen's Guard
> Song of Triumph ... Miss Ethel Condon
> Queen's Address ... Miss Lottie Smith
> Braiding of May Pole ... Junior Pupils

The above program was beautifully rendered, the pupils acquitting themselves in the most creditable manner of the different parts assigned to them.

The May Queen, whose noble bearing and style of delivery was wonderful in a child of 11 years, deserves special mention. Her address was as follows:

My Beloved Subjects,

It is with pleasure that I address you on this beautiful May morning. It is many years since a Queen has been crowned by such bright, loving hands in my grandpa's beautiful grove. Perhaps not since the time of the fairies; where I am sure they must have chosen this beautiful spot to hold high revels and dance in the moonlight with their charming King and Queen; but I do not think the fairies were half so good, lovely and faithful as my dear subjects. I have taken great pains to make this day of long-to-be-remembered pleasure for you, and I wish to see you enjoy it fully.

Any favor that I am able to grant you will be a pleasure, and, my dear subjects, I will take into consideration your many needs, especially for the time when you will desire to place your ballot in the box for our new President and will require the use of the bicycle to bring you in haste to the place of meeting, for I am determined that none of my dear subjects shall be behind the times, and very lately, I have heard that a young gentleman in Vallejo has invented a flying machine, and I will get one for you in order that you may visit Smith's Grove any time you desire to do so. Now be very happy today, the anticipation of all the good things provided for you, and those in store to come, should make you very happy. So one and all away and enjoy yourselves.

Capt. Anson has every reason to be proud of his well-drilled soldiers, who, seeming to imbibe his spirit of enthusiasm, carried the day.

Master Arthur Dunn in full costume made a gallant little captain and acted his part in an admirable manner.

After lunch Rev. Father McKinnon in his usual genial manner returned thanks to those present for their kindness, attention, etc., and was heartily applauded.

Judge H. Smith, the owner of the grove, also, we understand, gave the free use of the grounds to the pupils of the academy and did everything to add to their comfort, all in honor of the beautiful May Queen, who is his charming little grand-daughter, and really he has reason to be proud of so bright and promising a child.

-A Witness

Fruit crate label from Rio Vista, circa 1910, where Lottie attended school with Mabel Ruble of Ruble Orchard. (Author Collection)

CHAPTER 8

The Story of Josephine and Marcellus

1901

I write this story for all the Josephines and Marcelluses of the past and to come. May they find freedom and many places to belong. May they be able to meet their students' eyes with ease and pride. May they all be able to know deep in their hearts the conviction that love is just love. And may they always be cherished by all the people they meet. This story was told to my mother by my grandmother, Lottie Smith.

Lottie Smith

St. Gertrude's Academy for Girls, Rio Vista, California
~January 22, 1901~

The girls already knew. When the sisters told them what had happened, the girls knew that sometimes even nuns lie. In retrospect it was so obvious. Sister Marcellus and Sister Josephine were always friends. They could be seen walking arm in arm in the hallways of the Academy at lunch, after school and even at breaks. The hall monitors would whisper to themselves about it so often that it made Lottie and Laura laugh to think that those mere hall monitors thought they were so perceptive—as if, in retrospect, the rest of the high school girls hadn't put two and two together.

When Sister Camillus came to address the whole student body at Monday's noon assembly, she told the students in her calmest voice that Sister Marcellus and Sister Josephine were taking an unexpected vacation and may not return this year. There arose from the student body a high-pitched gasp, from the first graders all the way to the twelfth-grade seniors. "What? They're our favorites! What will we do for fun now? Where did they go? Why did they leave us?" All these thoughts and many more could be heard amid the chattering girls.

Lottie and Laura glanced wide-eyed at each other. Laura's eyebrows rose up and Lottie's blue eyes grew even wider. After all, they were juniors and this was 1901, a whole new century. The 1800s were past them. These were girls who were sure they knew something about the world.

"I knew it!" Lottie proclaimed.

"But to leave, Lottie!" Laura replied. "Where did they go? Do you think Camillus is mad at them?"

"I thought they were all friends," said Lottie.

The nuns at St. Gertrude's Academy had been a part of Lottie's growing up for so long that she couldn't imagine anything able to shake their world like this. But it shook all the girls for a while, and the nuns too. Lottie could see it in the way they taught classes for the next few months. They were not really talking about Marcellus and Josephine, but all the sisters were more silent, pensive.

Now, Lottie had trusted Sister Camillus from that first school day so long ago when she was eight. Camillus was her other parent, as much as Garrett and Marie Louise. But she knew that Camillus wasn't married like Mama and Papa were married. She knew the sisters never went on dates or had any men visitors. They were too old anyway for that, she told herself. But just this year she had begun to wish that there would be dances with the boys from St. Joseph's Military Academy across the way sometimes. She had even asked Camillus about it.

"Sister, why can't we have just one dance at the end of the year for the juniors too? It's not fair that only the seniors get the graduation dance. We should have one too, don't you think?" she asked nonchalantly.

"Now, Charlotte, we have talked about this many times. Junior girls are too young to have dances."

"But Sister, it's the 1900s! Why, last summer at Walnut Grove we had a hayride and all the girls and boys piled on the hay wagon. It was so much fun! And nothing happened, honest. Now don't you think it would be grand to have a little afternoon tea with the boys, just so we could meet them socially?"

Sister Camillus raised her eyes in silent prayer to this new God of the 1900s. She knew Lottie Smith was one of the smartest, brightest young girls she had seen at the Academy. And she knew Lottie would try her best to talk her into seeing the St. Joseph Academy boys on St. Gertrude's campus, one way or another. But Camillus would not be swayed. The graduation dance was enough, what with all that birds and bees nonsense. Last year she had even caught one of the girls kissing a young man behind the bandstand. How could she ever raise proper young ladies with two dances a year?

"Lottie, there will be no more discussing this. You can look forward to your senior dance and that's it. Now get back to work on those declensions and then we can practice your recitations."

So Lottie ended her inquiries about the dance. She had learned from Camillus's tone when enough was enough. That discussion was in November. Life at St. Gertrude's went on as it usually did, a settled routine for students and nuns alike: math and English studies in the mornings, painting and elocution in the afternoons. Study hall after dinner.

But then came January, and it was bitter cold that year. 1901 had already experienced record low temperatures for the Sacramento Valley. The snow piled up in the Sierra Nevada Mountains day after day. The river water was ice cold and there were several hard frosts at the school. On some mornings the girls awoke to a light dusting of snow. The whole school looked like the winter wonderland they'd been caroling about at Christmas with their own families, just last month.

It was January 22 when Camillus made her lunchtime announcement. There was no rhyme or reason to her explanation of the two nuns taking a vacation that the girls could see. Their absence was felt greatly, especially among the younger ones, the twelves and thirteens. "Where did they go? Why did they leave? Don't they have to do what Camillus tells them? She sure looked sad when she told us, don't you think?" The younger girls pestered all the high schoolers with their questions over the winter.

Female couple, 1890s (Private Collection, Sarah Shreeves, Flickr)

Even though the high schoolers were pretty sure that Sister Josephine and Sister Marcellus were in love, they also couldn't imagine it, really. Lottie and Laura had heard of it before, and when their two most popular nuns vanished, Laura said, "I'll bet Camillus kicked them out, Lottie, because she found them together!"

"Together where—in bed in the convent?"

"Yes."

"Well, I don't see how. They all have their own rooms," Lottie replied. Now, she had seen cows, sheep, and horses on her Papa's farm ever since she was small. She'd asked Marie Louise why they were stuck together sometimes. Her mother had told her that it was their way of making babies. Of course the little girl went on to ask if people made babies this way too. Marie Louise said something to the effect of a cursory yes and told Lottie that the time for that talk was when she was older.

Like most girls of the late Victorian age, Lottie never had that talk with her mother, Marie Louise. And like most young people of that time, she found out about sex from her peers. The girls had traded information back and forth since they were eleven or twelve. They shared things they'd heard from the boys or the public-school neighbors in the summertime, or what they'd read in farm books. However, Laura's mother had developed a new and interesting reading habit that Laura had discovered last summer—the dime romance novel. By reading these, they found out what adults really did, at times equally shocked and fascinated as they turned the pages.

"Oh my God!" Lottie exclaimed. "Let me read that again. Can you believe it, Laura?"

"Well, I guess all the married people must like it, otherwise why would they write about it so much in all these stories?"

"I mean, I can see kissing boys and all, but the rest is not what I'll ever do. No matter what!" Lottie firmly declared.

That conversation took place in the pear orchard behind Laura's house during their eighth-grade summer. It would be just seven years later that Charlotte Smith Lynch would deliver her first of seven children. She became a bride at nineteen and remained married to Philip Lynch for the next fifty years.

All her life, my grandmother Lottie liked to read all sorts of novels, never forgetting her first exposure to true romance. She told the tale of Josephine and Marcellus to her daughter Barbara several times. She remembered the two nuns abruptly leaving St. Gertrude's that winter of her junior year. And she told Barbara that once back in 1914, right after her thirtieth birthday, she remembered walking into Macy's in downtown San Francisco, where she saw the two nuns now dressed as ladies, walking side by side.

"Why, there's Josephine and Marcellus," she remembers saying aloud to no one at all. She looked right at them, hoping they would remember her too.

They walked right past her, not looking up. They could not meet her eye. Charlotte re-

Penny portrait of photographer Alice Austen and Gertrude Tate, a female couple of the time, circa 1905 (Courtesy of Alice Austen House)

membered feeling sad that they could not look at her. She felt strange for them and wistful too, remembering why they had left. All that day and every now and then she would remember that encounter and wonder about them and their lives together.

Now Lottie's story of those two nuns at St. Gertrude's Academy in Rio Vista has been written down. It's a full century later. I am Lottie's granddaughter. I live with my wife, Carolyn Brigit Flynn, whom I know Lottie would have liked very much. Carolyn and I had a grand wedding on March 11, 2007, with both of our families and many friends attending. My brother Pat Mahoney, a San Francisco judge, legally married us on July 4, 2008.

It should be noted that San Francisco was the first town in the United States to grant same-sex weddings, in February 2004, when then-Mayor Gavin Newsom asserted that the California Constitution's equal protection clause gave him authority to grant same-sex marriage licenses. In June of 2015 the United States Supreme Court agreed, ruling that same-sex marriage would be legal in all fifty states.

Lottie graduated St. Gertrude's Academy in 1902. She kept her commencement program in her scrapbook. My talented grandmother, who loved to perform, was featured four times during the commencement ceremony. Note that Miss Lottie Smith gave a recitation, played a part in the drama "Calpurnia," played an instrument, and was awarded a prize as top elocutionist.

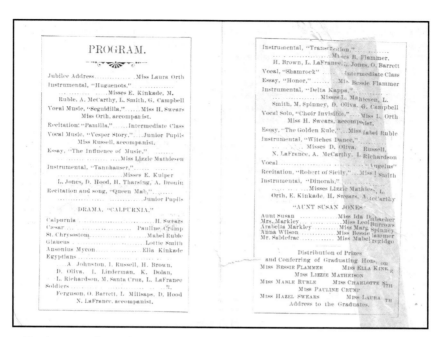

Charlotte Smith Lynch commencement program, St. Gertrude's Academy, 1902
(Charlotte's scrapbook, Author Collection)

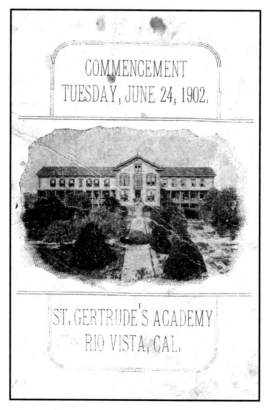

Cover of Charlotte Smith Lynch commencement
program, 1902 (Charlotte's scrapbook,
Author Collection)

PART THREE

San Francisco at the Turn of the Century

1902-1915

CHAPTER 9
Lottie Moves to The City
1902

Every living thing has a story. It is the story of their life.

Lottie moved to San Francisco right after she graduated high school. She wanted to be in the theater: to act, to elocute, to entertain on the stage. After her years at St. Gertrude's Academy for Girls in the hills of Rio Vista above the farmlands of the Sacramento Delta, Lottie thought—no, felt— she was ready for big city life.

After all, she'd been to San Francisco so many times before, in the summers between her boarding school years. Her whole family would sail downriver on the overnight steamship toward the cool San Francisco fog and get away from the summer heat in Isleton.

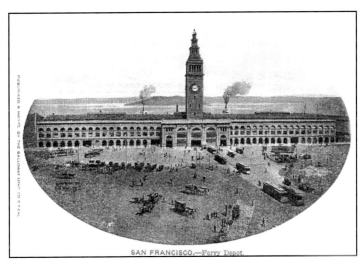

Postcard, San Francisco Ferry Building, 1898 (Author Collection)

65

Lottie's father Garrett Smith could leave the ranch for a few days at a time, with his foreman in charge. The whole family boarded the ferry bound for the City, their bags packed with summer clothes for the occasional warm days. Garrett and family would arrive: his wife Marie Louise, Lottie, his oldest daughter, Veda, his second daughter, and Hart and Warren, his two young sons. The ferry would dock at the shores of San Francisco Bay and the six of them would disembark at the Ferry Building, bound for Marie Louise's sister Amy's boarding house at 610 Larkin Street. Amy was Patrick and Anna Anson's fourth daughter. Unlike her sister Marie Louise, Amy had never left San Francisco.

"Right on time," Garrett would say as they pulled in to the dock, "we're right on time." He put his gold pocket watch back into his vest, buttoned his coat against the cool of the morning air, and led his family to the cable car.

Market Street, San Francisco, Detroit Photographic Co., 1900 (Library of Congress)

They'd board, Marie Louise holding gently onto her plumed hat, the girls' polished lace-up shoes stepping up on the outside ledge of the car. "Hold on, now!" the driver shouted, and they began their quick ascent up Market Street, almost two miles to Larkin Street. On the way, Lottie always noticed the street names: Montgomery, Kearny, Grant, Stockton, Powell, Mason and Hyde, until they finally came to the three-story boarding house on Larkin.

Of course, it was a great comfort for Lottie's mother Marie Louise to spend time in the City, where she had grown up and gone to school. It was easy to stay for a few days with her sister Amy in the boarding house and enjoy all San Francisco had to offer. On their summer sojourns, Lottie and her sister Veda accompanied Garrett to the Italian bakery on Sunday mornings. Garrett always bought them puff pastry with the powdered sugar on top. He let both girls eat their treats on the benches in Washington Square Park. With the smells of the bakery goods wafting from the sky, mingling with the tang of fresh-baked sourdough bread, San Francisco was, for Lottie, close to heaven. It's one of the reasons she resolved that when she turned eighteen she would come to live in the big city and become an actress. Now her dreams were finally being realized.

Lottie Smith

~August, 1902~

Lottie stepped from the ferryboat that summer day in 1902 ready for the world. Her trunks were packed for a long stay. The oil paintings and charcoal drawings from her time at St. Gertrude's were stored back in Isleton. Her graduation medal for elocution was tucked safely away for this journey, wrapped in the handkerchiefs her mother had hand-embroidered for her. She was eighteen years old, sure of herself, and set firm with her decision to live in the City with Aunt Amy and Uncle Joe.

Lottie's red hair blew in the morning while the City's foghorn sounded deep into the misty air. She and her mother Marie Louise scanned the crowd at the back of the newly built Ferry Building, looking for Aunt Amy's horse and buggy.

"Amy, Amy here we are!"

Aunt Amy waved her handkerchief high while her husband Joe nickered the horse toward her favorite niece.

Lottie ran, her long city dress flowing behind her. "Aunt Amy, Uncle Joe, the ride was lovely, the dolphins greeted us as we got to the shore. Do you have my room ready? How many other boarders are there? Can I really cook during the day and go to the theater at night?"

"Slow down, Lottie, all things in good time," Amy said as Joe urged the team toward home.

They trotted past City Hall and into the familiar neighborhood. When they reached the three-story boarding house, Lottie sighed and breathed in deeply.

"Aunt Amy. This is my life now, here in San Francisco."

As she stepped off Amy's buggy that Sunday morning, one of Amy's boarders reached for her trunk.

"I'm Philip," he announced.

"Lottie Smith."

"I know," he said. He carried her trunk easily up the stairs to the second-floor room, fixed up just for her.

Their courtship lasted seven months. Philip Lynch was twenty-six years old and had grown up in Brentwood on the east side of the Delta. Philip's parents, Ellen and Philip Lynch, had immigrated from Ireland, and owned a large farm where Phil had grown up. He'd lived in the City for six years, and now showed Lottie San Francisco. They rode horses out to Ocean Beach and went swimming at Sutro Baths. They took Phil's horses and brass-trimmed buggy all over town, up hills and down, and into the forest at Lake

Merced. Philip had the valet at the Hotel Majestic park the buggy around the back when they would go out for an after-theater dinner.

Philip had come to San Francisco to take over his Uncle Pat's hay, grain, and coal business, which was now going well. He had the means to court Lottie in an elegant manner. All those years at St. Gertrude's Academy had schooled her in the fine arts of dining, tea, oil painting, and of course, the theater. Lottie tried to hold tight to her dreams of acting and elocution, but she was so taken by the stars in Philip's eyes that her dreams of a starring role in the theater subsided for a time. They were married February 22, 1903, at St. Dominic's Church at the corner of Bush and Steiner. All their family came to the City. Lottie's parents Garrett and Marie Louise, along with her sister and brothers, made the sail downriver from Isleton. Philip's parents and several of his eleven brothers and sisters arrived from Brentwood. Patrick and Anna Anson, Lottie's grandparents who had first come to San Francisco from Muscatine, Iowa almost forty years before, were happy to attend the wedding of their firstborn granddaughter. Marie Louise sewed Lottie's beautiful light blue wedding gown by hand. They hired a photographer to capture the moment. The hills and vistas of San Francisco were now home to the next generation, the beautiful young couple Charlotte Smith Lynch and Philip Lynch.

Philip and Lottie took a train to Santa Cruz for a grand honeymoon. They enjoyed the Boardwalk and the shops on Pacific Avenue, while staying at the St. George Hotel. On their way to Santa Cruz they spent one night in San Jose, because Lottie was eager to see the "The Little Duchess" at the Victory Theatre. It was a "musical potpourri" featuring the famous French singer Anna Held, presented by the New York producer Florenz Ziegfeld, Jr. This fabulous international production featured specially designed evening gowns and hats selected by Mr. Ziegfeld in Paris. Lottie loved the extravaganza and found that her dream of acting on the stage remained vibrant and alive. Philip, too, was taken by the production's splendor. He saw his new wife safely tuck the theater program, titled "Figaro", in her suitcase and later paste it in her scrapbook, rekindling her love for the theater, which would continue for the rest of her life.

Victory Theater program for the play "The Little Duchess," San Jose, February 24, 1903 (Charlotte's scrapbook, Author Collection)

Philip and Charlotte Lynch wedding day, February 22, 1903 (Author Collection)

CHAPTER 10
Train Wreck

My grandmother Lottie, in her way, was sentimental. Over the years she told many stories of her life to my mother Barbara. My grandmother was proud of the medal for elocution she won in high school for her talent in the art of reciting long poems and solo essays in dramatic ways. I have saved this medal for my daughters, who are teachers and great elocutionists themselves. My grandmother saved things in her scrapbook: clippings, newspaper articles, photographs, theater pamphlets and cards from her times. These were things that changed her and shaped her life. My mother also saved my grandmother's old brown scrapbook, and passed it on to me. It is dog-eared and tattered, as things that you found in your childhood hall closets tend to be. But I have saved it all these years.

I am holding the very things my grandma cut out so long ago, family news clippings and stories of herself. I hold these messages right now. They are directly from her, saved for me to tell you about her life and times. Her stories have been roaming around in my head for a few years now. The one I am about to tell you came to me by way of a large cut-out page directly from her scrapbook, the front page of the *San Francisco Chronicle* from Tuesday, June 23, 1903. Its banner headline shouts out in one-inch letters: **RIDE OVER THE HILLS GIVES FRIGHTFUL AGONY TO UNFORTUNATE VICTIMS OF POINT REYES WRECK**; and underneath in slightly smaller type, the paper still shouts **DEAD AND DYING STREW THE GROUND**.

Now you who are reading this can read the entire two-page account on your own or you can search the internet for the details of this story that once garnished three full pages of the daily *San Francisco Chronicle*, the *Call Bulletin* and the *Marin Journal*. But I am going to tell this chapter of my grandmother's life with more detail than the *Chronicle*. This is one that shaped her life, and she looked at things afterward with different eyes. From her point of view, I will tell the before and after and during of my grandmother's experiences on that train, on that long summer solstice day.

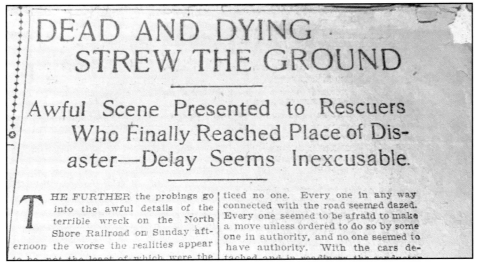

San Francisco Chronicle, Tuesday, June 23 ,1903 (Charlotte's scrapbook, Author Collection)

Lottie Lynch
~Sunday Morning, June 21, 1903~

I thought we might be late for the ferry. It left so early for a Sunday morning. Phil and I had agreed to go with Aunt Amy and Uncle Joe to old Mr. Dutton's funeral. We felt obligated to help pay our family's respects at his final resting place in Tomales, north of Point Reyes. Mr. Dutton was a pioneer and all, arriving as he did way back in 1849. Uncle Joe and Aunt Amy knew him well and wanted to be with his family at his burial. Uncle Joe was the dredger captain of Mr. Dutton's Bay fleet in the Delta. Of course, Mr. Dutton knew my mother and father, too. Why, he had been living close to my family's original home on Grizzly Island Ranch with his brother, after he retired to the Delta. He was seventy-seven years of age when he passed away. I could not imagine being that old!

Uncle Joe told me that Warren Dutton was the founder of the town of Tomales, and he and Samuel P. Taylor even helped start the narrow-gauge railroad all the way into Tomales in 1874. Uncle Joe and Mr. Dutton had such a long relationship with all the hauling and shipping between Marin County, San Francisco and the port in Sacramento. It seemed like Uncle Joe was always talking of dredging the Delta to keep the channels clear for produce boats at Suisun Bay. He and Mr. Dutton became close in business, and my husband Phil's hay, grain and coal business depended a lot on Mr. Dutton's shipping business as well.

It wasn't going to be a Catholic service, but that was fine. I didn't see how Phil and I could've done the 6 am Mass. We just told Mother we'd gotten a dispensation for the burial. As it was, I'd just laced my boots, pinned on my hat and gotten the breakfast dishes done. Since we moved to our flat at 72 Willow Avenue after our wedding four months ago, we had to make a short stop around the corner to pick up Amy and Joe at the boarding house on Larkin Street.

Phil drove us all up Market Street towards the Ferry Building. As the carriage clipped along, I said, "Why, it's June 21ˢᵗ and today's the first day of summer! Well, it'll be the longest day of the year, so surely we'll be home way before dark."

Phil and I were still both tired from last night at the theater. We saw "Her Majesty" at the Alcazar. I was so glad Philip liked it as well as I did. Why, I felt I could have done any one of those female parts. I did so love the theater. I promised myself I would keep trying to get an audition. I knew my destiny lie there. Even though we'd just married, I still wanted to be onstage.

My dear husband thought it was a grand idea as well, but I also knew that I was his wife and my job was to cook and clean, make a nice home for us. He was such a steady man, been at Lynch Hay, Grain and Coal there on Larkin Street for six years already. I did hope our life together would be grand. It's funny I fell immediately in love—head over heels—with the first man I met when I came to live in San Francisco. You never know what will happen, do you? You just never know.

When we met that day in 1902, he swept me off my feet! I was barely out of high school in Rio Vista. St Gertrude's had been my whole life for my last eight years and now I was married. To think that the sisters wanted me to be a nun! But I knew that was not my fate, even though I loved learning. I decided to leave the hot weather of the Delta behind and make my life in San Francisco.

Now that I had gotten closer to one year in the City, I knew my way around. I determined to make more time to get auditions. What with my talent for elocution and memorizing, perhaps I could present soliloquies to society the way I did when I was but a girl. Oh, but that was way back then. My life was here now with Philip, and even though he was six and a half years my senior, he still had a young man's twinkle in his eye. And he was such a kind, gentle man. Our age difference was good, I thought. He steadied me when I got too ambitious.

"We're almost there, Lottie," Phil said. "Let me take the horses to the Ferry Building stable for our return. We'll take the early train home from the Tomales Bay station. I suspect we'll get back home by dinnertime."

The ferryboat ride to the Sausalito train station was quick enough. I liked the new steamer they had, all wood panel and gold trim. I sat comfortably on the red velvet seats and enjoyed looking at the coastal scenery. Amy and Joe were pensive, as I imagine one

The ferry "Sausalito" between San Francisco and Sausalito, circa 1900
(A. Dickenson and R. Graves, *Narrow Gauge to the Redwoods*, 1981)

might be at the thought of such an important man's passing. Then we boarded the special funeral train to Tomales, which was relatively on time as well. As we made our way up White's Hill in Marin, I marveled to Aunt Amy how they built those trestles to climb so high. It took a lot of steam and strength to pull that train. The mood was somber on the way up, so much the opposite of picnic trains that I'd ridden on before. On those other trains there were children laughing, women wearing all colors of hats and dresses chatting and sharing recipes, men smoking and laughing in the parlor cars. But this train just did its job quietly. Carried us all dressed in black somber clothes across Richardson's Bay and through both of the tunnels in White's Hill, down into Point Reyes and on into the town of Tomales. By the time our little "narrow gauge" (as Phil called it) arrived, we were greeted by the carriages to take us up the hill to the church and Mr. Dutton's final resting place.

It was warm that day for Tomales, but not at all unbearable. The internment prayers at the gravesite were short. The Dutton's home was beautiful, high on the hill of California Street in Tomales. We visited, and consoled the family. In a couple of hours, Phil checked his pocket watch. "Gather up Amy and Joe. The train conductor told me they're putting on a special single car train for us in Tomales. We'll run ahead of the picnickers and be back home before the crowds. The train is scheduled to leave at 2:30. We have to hurry."

I glanced once again over at Mr. Dutton's two sons. They looked so forlorn now that the funeral was ending. How would that feel, I wondered, to lose your family? To look death itself right in the eye? My thoughts fluttered away, as there was a train to catch. Phil made sure the stagecoach driver was safely driving us down that hill. My new husband, after all, did have a very good sense of horses, speed and fast motion, after spending all his early years on the Brentwood ranch. Phil knew when to take it easy to slow down on the curves.

When we got to the Tomales Train Station, I could see that we would be in just the one small car hooked up to that big engine. Some of the funeral attendees decided to take the next train in order to enjoy the town of Tomales and have lunch there. All they seemed to be serving were oysters, shrimp, that type of fare. I just couldn't bear to eat shellfish, it didn't agree with me. "Let's just get home, Lottie," said Phil, and I readily agreed.

We boarded the only car, pulled by Engine Number 4. Aunt Amy and I settled into our seats mid-coach, with Phil and Joe next to us. The train started with a deep, low whistle. I never minded the trips we took by train. They were so fast and efficient and got you there comfortably. I could not stomach a long horse carriage ride, now that the trains traveled so easily up and down the coast. There were not too many passengers in the lone funeral car, enough to barely fill it, mostly older men and women and one little girl about eight years old who was the only child aboard. I overheard Phil and Joe talking about the Northwestern Railroad lines' plans to go electric. Now that would be something to see. They would add a third rail line, and run these engines up and down these mountains without the aid of a wood fire. This new century was bringing us into itself so fast. What would they think of next?

The train began our ride back to Sausalito, to pick up the ferry to San Francisco. Ten minutes into the ride, we passed the new Point Reyes station. I remember Aunt Amy saying that their Emporium was a good one.

"Maybe we'll stop there next trip, Lottie," she said. "And of course I will be more cheerful then. I know you didn't know Mr. Dutton well at all, but it was sweet of you and Phil to accompany us on this sad day. You know, you've

Northbound train on S-curve trestle over Papermill Creek, near Point Reyes Station, early 1900s (A. Dickenson and R. Graves, *Narrow Gauge to the Redwoods*, 1981)

got a good one in Phil. I knew him those couple of years at my boarding house, before you came to live with us. I know how solid he is. Lucky for you he decided to come to the City. He is not one for the farm life up in Brentwood, Lottie."

"Neither am I, Aunt Amy, neither am I," we both laughed, as the train ascended the hill towards Paper Mill Creek. Phil and Joe went out for a smoke on the platform. I noticed Phil's forehead was furrowed as he went out with Joe.

"Everything all right?" I asked.

"Just fine, dear, just fine. He's running it bit too fast for my liking."

As we rounded the summit of the hill, on the downward side of the mountain now, I had to hold onto my seat, passing the curves. Aunt Amy began to shout, "Whoo!" as we rounded each turn faster and faster. I held onto my hat and began hoping that Phil would get back in. They opened the door and almost stumbled into their seats.

"Here, let me sit by Amy," Joe declared. "Phil, you go next to Lottie. He's moving this train too fast and we're coming on to the trestle."

"I think we're going to crash and be dashed to pieces!" yelled Amy.

"Not on your life!" Joe shouted as he held onto his wife.

"Oh, Phil!" I screamed and gripped his arm tighter. No sooner had I said my husband's name but I felt the wheels strike the rail right and left and suddenly we were all hurtling downwards, overboard off the tracks! I closed my eyes and saw my mother's and father's faces as we tumbled through the air. The noise of the car crashing onto the ground was one I will

Train wreck survived by Charlotte and Philip Lynch, overturned single car, June 21, 1903 (A. Dickenson and R. Graves, *Narrow Gauge to the Redwoods*, 1981)

never forget as long as I live. I will always wish I never heard that sound. My whole body was sailing and crashing at the same time. People were screaming and crying out! I braced myself against Phil for the terrible landing and then it came with a screech, the crashing sound of metal, crunching of timber and wailing of passengers—all of us turned upside down! For one brief moment there was an eerie silence when not a word was heard, just the hiss of steam from the engine, a sighing really, that the worst of the damage was all over now.

I opened my eyes and what I saw is burned in my memory. I was pinned upside down underneath the seat I'd been sitting on, and Phil was too.

"Are you all right, Lottie?"

"Yes...yes, Phil I think so. How will we get out?" I moaned.

It was as if we were in a dream, and to this day I do not know whose hand stretched out to move the timbers from above us but I gladly took it. Both of us were helped up over the seats; I went first and Phil followed behind. I saw the light of day as I got on top of what used to be the floor and realized that I could not by myself have climbed out of that nightmare. There was blood on my dress, on my hat, and my arm was bruised and cut, but as I moved I felt that my bones were all in place.

Phil was next to me, his face gashed and his left hand red with blood.

"Oh Lottie!" he exclaimed. We just held on to one another, our mouths agape, our shoulders shuddering. It was then that I began to hear the moans and cries of the rest. This was a day I would never forget and pray never to live again.

I chanced to look around at the state of the others sprawled on the hillside. They were strewn about like ragdolls, really. Hoping to spy Amy and Joe, I looked for signs of them, their clothes, her hat, and listened to hear their voices. I could not see them at all.

"Phil, Amy and Joe are still in the car. We must go to them!"

"I will go, Lottie. You stay right here. I can get up. Can you move at all yet?"

"Yes, I think so. But Phil, your face!"

He wiped his cheek with his coat. "It's done bleeding." The gash was only a cut and was beginning to close. "Stay, Lottie, make sure you are able to breathe. Do not get up. Oh, my dear Lord," he whispered. He steadied himself on me, then walked a few paces and realized he'd better sit still, too. We were together, what a blessing that was!

All around me people were moaning and crying. I realized then that most of the passengers were much older than we were, maybe in their forties and older, being the mourners of their old friend. As I look back on it now, my age being almost nineteen years old and Phil just twenty-six helped us that horrible day. Yet as it was, I was in a deep state of complete and overwhelming shock at our fate! Although my body was strong, my mind remained in shock. I was not able to move about at first. Eventually I seemed to gather my wits about me, so I was able later on to help those worse off in that grief-stricken field, on that extraordinarily long afternoon.

And it was too long waiting, trying to help those in need. There was no next train to rescue us for hours on end. We lay there, all in a heap, really. A troop of Boy Scouts had heard the train from their camp below, and it seemed like about half an hour after the crash that they ran up to us with astonishment in their young, twelve-year-old eyes, and immediately began to help.

Finally, Joe and Amy got out of the train by the kindness of one of the Boy Scouts. We all sat stunned. I crawled to Amy and Joe. "Oh, Lottie, you and Phil are alive!" whispered Amy. Her body was limp where her rescuer had gently placed her beside Joe on the field.

Joe's right leg was bleeding through his pants leg. "Let me tie my shawl around your leg, Joe," I offered. Of course, there was no water to clean the wound, so I did my best to scrape the wooden splinters from his pants and skin, then tied my shawl on the upper part of his thigh, above the knee. The bleeding finally stopped and I was glad to be of some use to my family, but the cries of others surrounded us, to my horror.

Phil was one of the few younger men on the train. He and another man told the train's young fire tenders to run the mile and a half back to the Point Reyes Station to get help. You see, the engine was still on the tracks, and it was only our car that had flipped over and off the curve. Those two young men took off like jackrabbits, screaming, "Help! Help! Train wreck!" until they were out of sight. All we could do was wait for help. No telegraph, no telephone, just the strength of their young legs to carry the message of our peril.

It's strange how my body and mind worked rather well that long afternoon. Right after the crash, everything was as clear as day. It was like I was in a theater of horror, but this was real! Now my husband and I were surrounded in that field by dying adults, groaning women and men who lay stricken and bleeding, calling for help, praying for relief, dazed, confused, as only a tragedy such as this could bring us all to the brink of death.

As I said, the Boy Scouts heard the sounds of the wreck from their campsite a quarter mile away and ran up immediately. They were a welcome sight indeed. They had received training in basic wound care. Those boys were a godsend to us, bandaging wounds, running up and down the hill to get water from Paper Mill Creek. How they remained calm, I'll never know. Their scoutmaster must have been some kind of angel, as he kept them in line, and somewhat set a tone of wellbeing in the midst of this tragedy.

I got to wondering what time it was, though I knew by the sun's place so high above in the sky that it was late afternoon. I began to look for my watch locket that I had pinned on just this morning. No! My locket was not on my dress, not here above my heart. "Oh, no!" I whispered to no one but myself. "My father's locket is gone!"

Phil was next to me at that time. "What is it, Lottie?"

"My watch, the gold brooch from Benjamin Garrett, Phil, it's gone! I wore it on my wedding day, kept it dear to me ever since my blood father gave it to me six years past, you remember."

"I'll go back in the wreck and look," Phil whispered.

"No, no, no. You'll get hurt. Stay here with me. Help the others. Maybe it will turn up. We are safe and alive."

I touched his elbow, buried my face into his coat, cried a little, and a little more. Then I got my wits about me, gathered my strength and said again, "No, Phil, it's just a watch."

As it was, we did not return to San Francisco until 10 pm that night. All four of us and some other passengers on the train were brought straight to St Mary's Hospital. I was treated for shock and sent home in a few days.

In my later years, I have wondered about my brooch, whether it was stolen or lost in the ravine and the mess of that awful wreck. In the first months after the train disaster, I would miss it dearly when I wanted to know the hour. It was the only real thing my birth father, Benjamin Garrett, had given me. But as the years went by, there were so many other things to think about. Philip and I had our first son, Walter, just ten months later, in April of 1904. I was so busy that my theater plans were put aside. When I looked back on it, I realized that Phil and I were lucky to have escaped with our lives and limbs intact.

Life went on, but I never forgot that terrible summer solstice. It was a day that was burned in my mind, but we move on, don't we? We move on.

Newspaper coverage of Pt. Reyes train wreck with Charlotte and Philip Lynch listed as "injured and in shock." *San Francisco Call*, June 22, 1903.

I knew my Grandma Lottie until I was four years old. She is not that far away from me in my mind. In her times, as in my time now, there were train wrecks, accidents, really awful things that happened in the course of a lifetime. If you are lucky enough to survive them, you consider yourself blessed. But glancing back, you can still feel the horror, the panic you felt as your life rushed before your eyes. And you, lucky you, came out with eyes wide open on the other side. So, I re-read these 112-year-old newspapers, and see. See that a long life has these moments. Whether you are living in the nineteenth, twentieth or twenty-first century, life has these moments. Today, there are airplanes that go missing, cars that crash, terrible accidents that happen in spite of our cell phones, our airplane security checks, our speed limits. I just see. See that my people came through most of them, anyway, with their bodies and spirit intact. I see and feel as I go back into these stories that sometimes people have near-death experiences. Many of us today have been shaken with shock and fear. Writing this story, I see that my grandparents' strength, bravery and luck gives me hope. This insight gives me the gift that once again, every day here is precious to me, every life, every tree, each rock, each earthquake, each passing moment is unto itself wondrous and full. Wonderful.

CHAPTER 11
1906 Earthquake!

At 5:12 am on April 18, 1906, almost three years after the train wreck, the people of San Francisco were awakened by an earthquake that would devastate the city. The main temblor had a 7.7 to 7.9 magnitude, lasted about one minute, and was the result of the rupturing of the northernmost 296 miles of the 800-mile San Andreas fault. But the earthquake took second place to the great fire that followed. The fire lasted four days and most likely started with broken gas lines. With water mains broken, fighting the fires was almost impossible, and about 500 city blocks were destroyed. The damages were estimated at about $400,000,000 in 1906 dollars, which would translate to about $8.2 billion today.

In 1906, San Francisco was the ninth-largest United States city with a population of 400,000. More than 225,000 people were left homeless by the disaster. The death toll is uncertain. At the time, city officials estimated the casualties at 700. Yet modern calculations say about 3,000 lost their lives. The lowball city figures may have been a public relations ploy to downplay the disaster with an eye on rebuilding the city.

In 1906, my grandparents Lottie and Phil Lynch were living in a two-story house in the Richmond district of San Francisco. Phil's hay, grain and coal yard, from which he made his livelihood, was downtown, almost three miles away.

Combined *San Francisco Call-Chronicle-Examiner* earthquake coverage,
Thursday, April 19, 1906 (Library of Congress)

Lottie Lynch
~April 18, 1906~

When the shaking started that morning a little after 5 am, it threw me right out of bed! We both rushed to Walter's crib and Philip scooped up our toddler into his arms. We ran for the doorway; my mother had taught me this over the years. The shaking lasted for almost one full minute. The sound was horrifying—a gigantic boom from the ocean, and then the street lamps creaking and rolling, trees swaying every which way, dishes falling out of cupboards and chimneys falling, until the first waves stopped. The ground rolled beneath us and dropped us to our knees.

We drew in a breath. When the shaking stopped, it left us with an eerie silence and barely only dust to breathe, just as the light from the sunrise entered our bay window.

We looked at each other wide-eyed. We both held Walter close for several hours. Philip checked the house: my wedding china had crashed to the floor, part of the ceiling had collapsed, and outside, the chimney had fallen! There were no rains to speak of the first several days, so we stayed dry.

My husband and I both looked around to see what was still intact in the living room and the rest of the house, while Walter cried. I held him tight, glad for our lives. Lord in Heaven, let me tell you, I had never seen anything like this quake! Of course, we had small earthquakes when I was younger. Mama told me there had been a big shaker in 1884 when I was just born and we lived in the City. Yet up in the Delta when I was a young girl, we didn't feel earthquakes, why hardly at all. I knew they existed, of course, but nothing like this terror. First, the shaking went on for that minute, and I saw that all the water in our hall basin had splashed out to the floor. With all my china broken amidst the rubble, I thought, *This will be a grand mess to clean!*

After checking the house, we ran down the steps to see about Phil's horse. It was then that I realized that Phil would need to go downtown to see his business and check on the horses there. So I resolved in my mind to make do with staying alone for some part of that day.

Victorian frame houses tumbled from foundations, SF earthquake, by H.C. White Co., circa 1906
(Library of Congress)

After we saw that our horse outside the house was still tied to its post, Philip proposed we take the buggy up to Laurel Hill to see down to the bayside and downtown of the City. As I said, I felt he had to be going there anyway, so I wanted to see if he'd be safe. I dressed Walter in pants and a jacket, threw on one of my oldest dresses and a hat, and buttoned up my shoes. There was debris and rubble everywhere as we rode those few blocks up the hill. Some folks were already dressed and out of their houses. Chimneys were down everywhere, and some houses had glass windows fallen into the street. It was shocking to see that a few houses had tilted off their foundations and slanted into the houses next door.

When we got to the top of the hill, it was hard to tell what was going on downtown almost three miles away. The air was a thick gray and there were several fires below Market Street. I could see to the Ferry Building, and it was still standing and fine. But I could tell no more.

Later that afternoon Phil took his buggy downtown to check on the hay, grain and coal yard. I stayed with Walter. It was not easy with Phil leaving, but we both knew he had to go. He assured me he'd be back by sundown. I gathered my wits together and stepped once again inside our house, cautiously.

Walter was walking but still a toddler, and tended to put things in his mouth to see what tasted good. That was a challenge, to keep him out of the mess. I held onto him most of that day.

I didn't really feel safe indoors, especially since we had a two-story house and the shaking was so rough. After a quick inspection of the house, I grabbed some clothes and food for the rest of the day. Then I stayed outside talking with neighbors and exchanging information. Every few hours an aftershock came, rattling us all terribly. These were swift reminders of what we'd all just lived through. We all were in the same boat. Together we began to make plans for how to cook and get water. There was no running water in any of our pipes.

We slept fitfully in our own beds those first few nights after the quake. I wasn't sure at all if sleeping indoors was the right decision, but Phil seemed to think that since the house had held during the first terrible shake, it would hold again in the aftershocks. Besides, we didn't want to get hit by anyone else's falling bricks. Our sleep was not sound to be sure, but thank God that Phil was right and the house held together during the aftershocks. There were a few strong shocks on the first day, several the next day, then they tapered off over the weeks. By the third week or so, it seemed the earth had mostly settled back into itself, and things were calmer.

Let me tell you, we had a devil of a time getting the cast iron stove outside, about two weeks after the quake. It took three men to carry it down the steps to the sidewalk. Since the first day of the earthquake, I had cooked on a grate over an open flame. It was a relief to have my familiar oven and stovetop to prepare meals. The spring season was upon us and the weather was fair. The water pipes trickled out a little the first day, then nothing until water trucks arrived from many generous souls down on the Peninsula. Washing outside reminded me of days on the Delta, with no indoor plumbing, and of course I had to deal with the baby's diapers. I resolved to try to get Walter trained soon.

Cooking on the street after the earthquake, San Francisco, Detroit Publishing Company, 1906 (Library of Congress)

I realized a few weeks after the earthquake that my state of mind was similar to the way I had felt for months after the train wreck—why, that had happened to Phil and me almost three years before. Since then I'd become more cautious, wary, you might say. But this was different, because everyone in the City was in the same situation, and we all surged on with life. I kept telling myself, *Charlotte, you can't let the hard times take you over completely!* What a world this is. And then my thoughts would turn to how lucky we both were to survive one more disaster.

Once we got the stove down to the street, I could cook with relative ease. I knew how to stoke the fire with wood, having done that since my childhood on the Delta. Anyway, we couldn't cook inside until the chimney had been fixed and the inspector came, and that took almost a couple of months. Food supplies were interesting, to say the least. I was able to stand in the lines for fresh fruits and vegetables, along with the rest of the neighborhood women. We got what was offered, and made do. I was able to get staples as well: butter, sugar and flour. Meat, chickens, pork and such arrived on the boats on ice from folks who donated from northern Marin and Sonoma counties. Of course, everything fresh had to be cooked the day you received the rations.

I tried my best to document this disaster, of course. Oh, yes, I had a camera. A few of the families in our neighborhood had Brownie cameras. Mine was a little box of a thing. You held it in your hands, looked down through the view window, and snapped black and white photographs sharp and clear as anything. After the first few days of shaking, I tentatively gathered my wits about me and took photographs. I wanted to save this event for posterity as I'd saved other events in my life. Phil held the baby while we walked our small neighborhood, all of us still in a kind of stunned shock. It turned out that during

Refugee camp in Golden Gate Park after San Francisco Earthquake, 1906 (U.S. National Archives)

the month of April, after most of the shaking had stopped, I took a whole roll of pictures, including several photographs of the destruction around our house at Third and Clement, as well as pictures of the stores in our neighborhood. My camera caught the gray haze in the air from the fires downtown, just one week after our big quake. I could still see the smoldering ruins of the buildings on Van Ness Avenue as I was taking my photographs.

Smoke and ash filled the air for weeks, it seemed. Everywhere, there was destruction and sadness. Because we lived on the outskirts of town, I didn't see firsthand the devastation downtown the way Philip did. Aunt Amy and Uncle Joe had fled by ferryboat to the East Bay and lived safely in Alameda after that, until the day they died. We were so much more fortunate than those in the tent city over in Golden Gate Park. Their houses had burned or been shaken to the core, so they had nothing left but their few belongings, perhaps some clothes. Thousands of families who had to leave their homes were living below the park's panhandle, in tents or little cabins built by the government. Well, I thought, at least it's spring and the weather's all right. Not a lot of rain, and the fog cleared up by noon or so. A few weeks after the quake, once I'd seen my own house settled without too much damage, I walked Walter in his pram down to the park to help serve food to the folks standing in the breadlines there. I donated some of our clothes to them as well.

And you might be wondering, why can't you see my photos here? Well, I gave my photo albums to my first daughter, Camilla. She didn't save things like my youngest daughter Barbara did. One afternoon, probably in the 1960s, she was cleaning her attic and decided to give the photos to the Goodwill. Barbara did inquire about them later and Camilla told her that she didn't think anyone would want them, anyway.

Philip Lynch
~April 18, 1906~

It was a shaker, all right. All of us had settled into sleep that early morning of April 18, 1906. Even the baby was sound asleep. I woke with a start as soon as I heard the sound, more of a deep rumble and crack from the west—it felt like it was coming from over by the Farallon Islands. Then the shaking started. Lottie and I ran to get Walter from his crib. We ran for the front door, held on tight to the door frame, and then we couldn't stand. We fell to our knees for the rest of that interminable minute as I watched houses sway, young trees bend to the ground and chimneys topple across the street. I listened to the screams of neighbors and my own small family. The baby whimpered and we held him as tight as we could while the earth rolled beneath us. Our windows shook and rattled, the chandelier swayed, and across the street, our neighbor's glass-pane windows popped out of their frames and clashed to the ground. Then the shaking and rolling stopped. Amongst the dust, a calm, eerie quiet arrived that I will never forget. Even the birds were without song. Everywhere there was dust, broken windows, and plaster fallen from our roof, but at least our house was still standing.

I checked Lottie and Walter and we, all three of us, went outside to my horse and wagon. Living out here at the edge of town, I never took the trolley home, always the horse and wagon. My horse was shaken, pawing the ground and whinnying, but since I had tied him up good to the rail the night before (as is my habit), he was still there. I tried to quiet and calm him. I had never seen animals through anything quite like this. My wagon was fine, no worse for the wear at all. I figured that as soon as I could see my family was safe, I would take my cart and horse downtown to check on the yard. There were two horses there in their stalls for the night, along with my two other wagons for drayage.

I saw that my wife and I were wide-eyed once again. The shaking and terror we felt was akin to the shock we had withstood almost three years before in the train wreck. But we came out of that damn mess alive, as we did this. Everyone in the whole City seemed to be in quiet shock. After a while neighbors began to talk to one another, moving about the street, checking on one another. Everyone in our small block was all right, thank God. But children clung to their parents. Folks were in shock from the force and severity of the quake. I talked with my neighbor to see if he would watch over Lottie and the baby so I could be on my way downtown for a couple of hours that afternoon, what with my horses alone there. He warned me that he'd heard City Hall was in shambles—heard it from a young man who'd been sleeping in a flat on Market Street and ran up the Laurel Street hills to check on his elderly parents, who live in our neighborhood.

I was torn, to tell you the truth. My whole livelihood was downtown in the yard. I knew I had to take a look at the situation there, so after I made sure the three of us were okay, we decided to get a sense of the rest of the City. I placed my dear wife and son in the buggy and we rode the short climb up a few blocks to Laurel Hill. That way I could see downtown, try to size up things from there. Over to my right, on the south of town below The Slot near Mission Street, smoke was rising in several blocks. I guess a couple of folks decided to cook breakfast, and their broken gas mains had blown up. I hoped this would be small. Lord knows, a big fire could ruin the whole city!

Well, I had to get down to the yard that same day. After spending several hours at home, we agreed that Lottie and Walter would keep company with our neighbors. I promised I'd return by sundown. With that, I hitched my horse to the wagon and set off down the hills towards Larkin and Eddy, around the block from City Hall. On my way, I passed sights that startled, shocked and saddened me to this day. Buildings were thrown from their foundations. The streets were twisted and rose up and sank down from the aftershocks as I went. By this time, about I pm, folks were dressed and had come outside just to be with one another. As I look back on it, the whole town was in shock; no one

Ruins of San Francisco City Hall after earthquake. Only the dome survived. Detroit Publishing Co., 1906 (Library of Congress)

was exempt from this extreme quake to all of our senses. I thought, *Terra firma is no more.*

Since my buggy was empty, many folks ran up to me on my way and asked for rides. They wanted to pay me to carry their trunks and such downtown to the Ferry Building so they could get out of town and go across to the East Bay or Marin County. I told them I was going as far as City Hall, near where my business was. No need to pay me. The buggy was full of passengers by the time I got close to my fuel yard. There were so many streets that were not passable, it's a wonder I could wend my way to the yard. I think it was then that I realized what a damn mess this was. I came in through the back and checked my horses, who were still in their stalls, and I was relieved to see that my wagons were intact. I double-teamed two horses to my biggest wagon.

By this time there seemed to be more smoke than ever in the air and fires sprouted up close to me, just blocks away. Then and there I resolved to help out others, and do whatever rescue work was needed. That afternoon I dug out a few people from the rubble off Larkin Street, my horses beside me, helping pull away fallen walls and chimneys off those trapped by the scorn of nature's wrath.

I tried to take those folks to the Central Emergency Hospital over by City Hall, just two blocks away, but when I turned the corner, the hospital was gone! The quake and aftershocks had knocked it off its foundation and it was almost totally collapsed. The patients who had survived were being moved as quickly as possible to Mechanics Pavilion over on Grove and Larkin. I tried to get my charges into the Mechanics Pavilion as soon as I could, but that large meeting hall had its own disaster. Nearby fires had reached the Pavilion roof and that building too was going to go up in flames! What with the fires advancing and eating up blocks of the city at a time, all of us wore kerchiefs covering out faces to help us breathe. It was

Street scene after San Francisco earthquake, by Arnold Genthe, photographer, 1906 (Library of Congress)

hard to see in the haze, and I had to watch out for flying cinders.

I was directed by soldiers to drive my team and the patients in the wagon three miles from downtown to the Presidio Army base. I went by way of Van Ness Avenue over to Cow Hollow, to the emergency headquarters there at the Army base. Everywhere there were folks in need, some bleeding and moaning. I kept a cool head about me and soldiered on, wending my way through twisted streets. I helped the injured folks off the wagon and got them safely into the hastily assembled hospital quarters. I looked out toward the ocean and saw that the sun was beginning to set. I had promised Lottie to be home by dark. I urged my team from the Presidio, down Arguello, and back home.

I arrived home safely that evening, bone tired. I told Lottie that City Hall was a shambles—nothing left but the dome! She was anxious for news about Aunt Amy and Uncle Joe, who lived downtown. I told her I'd learned that they had taken a ferry across to the East Bay. I described how the front of Larkin was twisted and torn up, and that fires, as she could tell from the smoke beginning to thicken the sky, were everywhere—fires that wouldn't quit. I recounted my day, as she did hers.

Of course, we all slept uneasily those first few nights, and even weeks after the quake, but then in each morning's light we got up and started again.

Once I realized that downtown San Francisco was literally going up in flames, I set my sights on what needed doing closer to home, in our own neighborhood. Besides, I could not leave Lottie and Walter alone again. *Lord knows*, I thought, *what else could happen?*

Already we had to deal with the broken chimney, dishes scattered everywhere, and cracks in our roof. Lottie began cooking outside, at first just on the street, on a grate on top of an open fire pit the neighbors made from the fallen chimney bricks that lined the streets. We finally moved our stove to the street. We all shared what we had already in our iceboxes: butter, eggs, vegetables, etc. How we got water those first few weeks was a whole other story. Folks from far and wide sent help, including water trucks that arrived from the South Bay town of San Jose and several towns on the Peninsula. It took over a week before the reservoir was declared safe and water began to flow back into the house.

I realized that I had to stay with my family and close to home, but my team was available and set to help. I fed the horses with bales of hay that I had in the shed out back. Eventually I got word that my folks, brothers and sisters were getting on okay in the East Bay town of Brentwood. They were busy sending barges of hay down from the Delta to feed the

Spectators on hillside watch fires consume San Francisco after earthquake, by Arnold Genthe, April 1906 (Library of Congress)

City's livestock. Most all the buildings for blocks around my yard were ruined, but the land on the yard was clear and could still be used for storage of hay, grain, and coal. Folks still needed fuel—food for the horses, coal for cooking fires.

The original quake was on Wednesday, and the fires raged on until Saturday, when God finally sent rain to us and the fires went out. Soldiers had by then dynamited one side of the wide street of Van Ness Avenue. This line stopped the fires from marching over the whole city, all the way to the ocean. I started to think that I should relocate my hay, grain and coal lot to one of the lots I knew might be available now. Over the next months, I moved my horses, wagons and supplies to a lot on Seventeenth and Valencia, and then to Sutter Street. These locations made it easier for folks to get their fuel, as they were farther from the burned areas.

Regarding myself and my family, I realized as it turned out that we were some of the lucky ones. Let me tell you, some of the things I saw over that April and into May of 1906 left me shuddering in my bed at night for months afterward. I was young at the time. Our youth helped us, I think, to weather yet another disaster.

I began to think of a quieter life away from the City. So we moved to Lomita Park, on the Peninsula near Burlingame, a year and a half after the big quake. Got a fine house on Acacia Avenue, big enough for our growing family. My second son, Phil Jr., was born in San Francisco November of 1907, and Camilla came along two years later in April of 1909 in Burlingame. We had three more kids there, for a total brood of six. I still kept the hay, grain, and coal business downtown, and I had a bigger yard with my name attached to the lease. It was just a five-minute walk for me to the train station. I took the Southern Pacific train up the Bayshore route in the morning to San Francisco, and happily rode back to our home in the suburbs a little after 5 o'clock in the afternoon.

CHAPTER 12
The Taste of Sweet
1909–1915

There is something about the taste of sweet on the tongue. Something about going to bed every night for many nights, happy. Something you hold in your hand and put up to the light, admiring these times all the while. Something about seeing the delivery wagon carrying boxes of ripe pears, picked just yesterday morning, arriving on your doorstep, from your parents' farm on the Sacramento Delta.

Remembering the Delta air of your childhood home, so warm at night, so different from this air here on the San Francisco Peninsula, tinged as it was with sunshine in the daytime and cool with fog and ocean breezes in the evenings. Something about the rhythm of a happy time in life when children are well, and your husband has steady work. Times that provide you with time, you a busy mother, ironing the kids' school clothes, marveling at this new washing machine, wishing someone would invent a drying machine.

Time. Time to hold tea parties, to entertain your friends in the early afternoons when your children are in school. Time to go to market, buy fresh food, plan meals, and work hard in the kitchen cooking for your family. Then to have the time to elocute, to recite poetry with your friends or play in the evenings with the children, when the meals were cooked and the dishes done.

I think about my grandma and my grandpa, and I am happy to know of their years in Burlingame, when my grandfather focused on his business and their family was growing. Back then, the population of that small town of Burlingame was just 345 residents. In 1912 my grandmother was proud to be among the first women voters in their state election, as women gained legal voting status that year in California. It would be another eight years until Lottie could vote in a federal election.

My grandmother had time not only to raise her children, but also to star in community plays. She had time to entertain, just as she had been taught on the Delta, by the nuns at St Gertrude's Boarding School and her mother Marie Louise, all those years before.

The days on Acacia Avenue in Burlingame were golden years, really. Times when they savored their luck. Both of them always considered their six years in Burlingame to be blessed. Their first daughter, Camilla, was born there; then two more sons came along,

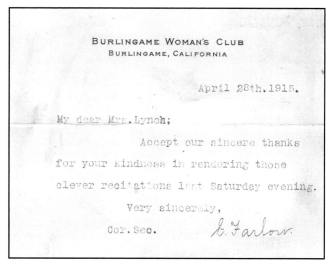

Letter from Burlingame Women's Club to Charlotte Lynch, April 1915 (Author Collection)

Donald and Jack. Finally, baby Russell was born on March 4, 1914. Russell caught the apple of all their collective eyes. My grandma thought that Russell would be her last baby. He was her last in Burlingame, until my mother, Barbara, was born in 1919 in the East Bay town of Alameda. But that's later on, in another town and in another chapter.

This one's about Burlingame: 824 Acacia Drive. I hold in my hands one of my grandmother's old cookbooks. I say "one of them" because she must have had many cookbooks, as she had been cooking every day since the beginning days of her marriage to Philip, then later, for all of her children and any relations that would show up at her table. This cookbook was published by the Crisco Company in 1913. The book opens right to her favorite pages, spattered with spots of sugar, butter and cream. The chapter heading is CAKES: Pound Cake, Caramel Cake, Chocolate Cake, Coconut Layer Cake, Hurry Up Cake, and on and on.

I imagine my grandfather walking up the front walkway in the evenings, opening the door and being greeted by his brood: six kids and their spaniel jumping on him. His wife Lottie would be in the kitchen, whipping up popovers or cakes by hand to go with dinner. Times were good on Acacia Avenue; they both knew it, and were grateful and so busy.

Charlotte Lynch cookbook, Crisco Company, 1913 (Author Collection)

Philip Lynch
~April 1915~

Phil was glad to see Lottie finally settled into one house now. After the quake, they had moved several times. She seemed anxious and upset easily after that shaker in '06. *Lord*, he thought, *everyone in the whole city was nervous and on edge, what with the aftershocks going for weeks, and all the folks in the neighborhoods cooking outside, afraid to go back inside for fear of another shaker!* But now they were on the Peninsula in a house, where they were finally settled with a long-term lease. Here Phil could feel the warmth of the sun of a regular basis, and he could still go hunting in the woods over by the Crystal Springs Reservoir. There were plenty of rabbits, deer, and quail to be found there and brought home for Sunday dinner.

Serving dessert, *Crisco Cookbook*, 1915
(Author Collection)

Lottie was, as always, an excellent cook. He was happy to earn enough to provide her with a little help, and occasionally they hired someone to assist with the day-to-day ironing and washing. But it was always Lottie who did the cooking and the shopping. Phil was glad of it, and grateful.

Lottie had the knack for putting together just the right meals for their growing family. Their table was set with full dinners as was the custom of the day: meat, fish or fowl, vegetable, starch, bread, butter and yes, dessert. Lottie was a wonderful baker. She loved the way you can plan the taste you want, then measure the ingredients, bake them to just the right degree and time, and voila! A splendid cake, pie or pan of cookies would appear, warm and ready for the family.

Lottie Lynch
~April 1915~

6:30 am. Lottie opened her eyes with anticipation. She'd been planning this day for months, and now, finally, it was here. Outside sun streamed into the windows, highlighting her bone china and tea sets. She'd had tea parties before, but this was her largest one yet. It would be elegant and fine. But there was a lot to do between now and one pm!

Philip stirred beside her. He never would understand all the work and planning that she put into her parties. He turned now and smiled to his wife. "Mother, I know it's your day. I hope it's all you want."

Lottie cupped Philip's face in her hands. "Thank you, Father. Now you better get moving or you'll miss your train!"

Philip grinned. "I know you just want to get me out from under your feet."

Lottie was pulling the coverlet up over the bed. "No, husband," she peeked over at him. But in truth, the answer was *yes*! She had much to do, and just then children and husband were not part of the picture. It didn't take long for the older kids to get dressed and soon they were out the door to school. Washing the breakfast dishes, she remembered what Camilla had said just as she left for first grade. "Mother, I really am old enough to help you with the party. I could wear my best party dress, and I won't eat too much cake!"

Lottie mused, *That daughter of mine, why I'll bet she'll grow up to be a fine lady herself. Nothing but the best for Camilla. Sometimes she just wants her way.* Then in her skilled, motherly way she helped one-year-old Russell out of his pajamas and into his sailor suit, hoping he would stay clean until lunchtime. Four-year-old Donald was busy getting himself dressed in his cowboy outfit, and Jack, just two years old, still needed her help to put on his shoes and socks. The doorbell rang and her two helpers arrived, one swooping Russell up in her arms and coaxing Jack and Don outside to play while the other set to work in the kitchen. Lottie was alone in the living room. She took a deep breath. She had just three hours.

Really, she was part of society now, and goodness knows, her neighbor George might even put an item in the paper afterwards! George Douglas, *San Francisco Chronicle* editor, was a true friend. His wife, Grace, would be in attendance. Lottie's heart fluttered slightly with anticipation. She took another deep breath. It would be lovely, a time for her and her friends to get dressed up and enjoy each other. She'd already chosen the pale pink color theme for the tables, polished the silver, and washed her fine wedding china with its delicate teacups.

She took her imported chocolate pot and the cookie plate down from the hutch, admiring its hand-painted gold touches surrounding the soft brush strokes of the artisans' handiwork of pink-and-white flower blossoms. This piece was one that she had purchased after the 1906 quake to replace some of her lovely things lost that year. She carefully set the silver octagonal tea holder on the sideboard. Lottie thought back to times with her mother, sharing tea on the Delta, and how the French nuns at St. Gertrude's Boarding School had trained her all those years, from grammar school into high school, on the nuances of refined behavior during teatime. Her mother also had shown Lottie how this was done, with her afternoon parties on the Delta, the ladies in their dresses and gentleman in their hats sitting outside in the shade of the sycamore tree.

Charlotte Lynch's chocolate pot
(Author Collection)

Now Lottie was a grown woman, thirty-one years old, and it would be a pleasure to share these treasures with good friends, treasures of cakes and sweets that she had enjoyed baking in the kitchen all week. She'd serve imported teas and hot chocolate from her chocolate pot, using lovely fine china and graceful table settings. The guests would enjoy each other's company and afterwards play whist and other card games. Thank goodness she'd been able to hire a little extra help for the day. Soon, with her helpers, the tables were set up and the place settings laid out.

Everyone had received Lottie's handwritten invitations for tea in their mailboxes and had cordially RSVP'd. She knew they would come. With an hour to go, Lottie changed into her new dress and smoothed her hair. She smiled into the glass. Her wavy red hair looked just fine today. She'd spent a little extra on the dress and hadn't told Phil yet. But now she turned in the mirror with approval. She'd chosen well on her last shopping trip to the City, and her dress was perfect. Now there were just the final moments of anticipation, feeling the house clean and everything prepared, three tables set up in the parlor, four settings to a table, with pale pink floral tablecloths and a fresh rose to each, and fresh flowers in the hallway.

Guests arrived wearing the latest fashions: long skirts, fancy hats, button-up boots and gloves. Lottie's younger sister, Veda, arrived with their mother, Marie Louise. Aunts Amy and Et came from the East Bay, and some of her own neighbors from Lomita Park attended. They all looked bright and fresh at her door.

Her guests played card games while exchanging tales of children, what so-and-so had been up to, and other news of the day. They raved about her fresh-baked sweets, and the delicious tea. By the end, she knew everyone had an enjoyable time. The next day, there was a notice in the society section of the *San Francisco Chronicle* about the successful party Mrs. Philip Lynch hosted. She cut this out and pasted it carefully in her scrapbook.

MRS. PHILLIP LYNCH HOSTESS TO FRIENDS

Mrs. Phillip Lynch was hostess to a number of her friends at a delightful afternoon at her home on Burlingame Terrace, Wednesday. Cards and fancy work were the diversion of the early part of the afternoon and later dainty refreshments were enjoyed. Mrs. Geo. Douglass won the first prize for cards. Those present were: Mesdames Paul Biber, M. H. Atkins, Frank Sabrelle, Geo. Douglass, J. J. Cook, of Alameda, Jos. Lynch of San Francisco, Fisher of Easton and Miss Vida Smith.

San Francisco Chronicle newspaper clipping of
one of Charlotte's tea parties, circa 1915
(Charlotte's scrapbook, Author Collection)

Philip Lynch
~April 1915~

Philip arrived at the Lomita Park train station that evening at 5:30 pm, coming from the express train that took just fifteen minutes to travel twelve miles from San Francisco's busy Third and Townsend station. He had a three-block walk to Acacia Avenue. As he stepped off the train, he breathed the air of a happy man. Fulfilled, really. This life was all he'd ever hoped for. He had a beautiful, smart, vivacious wife and six gorgeous, healthy children. He felt accomplished and proud for a man of thirty-eight years. His business was successful and coal was still plentiful. There were weekly shipments from the coal mines below Mt. Diablo, and Philip was able to supply his customers in the City with plenty of coal for heating and cooking. He liked being the boss of his own small business, always had. Those two years of business school at San Francisco City College had paid off. He had a good head for figures, anyway. Taking all this in, he turned his gaze up towards the Coast Range carrying in the afternoon fog and was glad to be alive in this new century. He pushed open the front gate to his family's home.

Just then, Camilla came bounding up to him. "The tea party was so much fun! Mama let me come to the last five minutes. I had to keep Jack and Don away from the cake, but the guests let us have some anyway! Come in and see the tables, Daddy, they look so pretty!"

"All right, Camilla. Let's go see!" He swooped her up in his arms, opened the front door, and saw Don and Jack running around the tables, playing hide and seek. Phil Jr. was stuffing himself with cake, and Walter was playing baseball in the yard. Russell, ensconced in his mother's arms, was crying, as babies often do at 5 pm.

"Hello, Father," said Lottie. She pecked him on the cheek, handed Russell over to him, and sat down. She happily told him all the events of the day.

"Sounds grand, Mother. I have been thinking. Let's take in the Panama-Pacific Exposition this weekend. I know we've been before, but we took the children then. There's so much more to see! We could leave our brood with the Douglases next door and go by ourselves, just like we used to before we had all these kids. What do you say?"

"Splendid, Phil. I'll get the map I cut out from the *Chronicle* when the exhibit first opened in February. Everything's all laid out there, so much to see and do. Look, there's even a little train that will take us all around. Oh, what fun, Phil!"

CHAPTER 13

The Panama-Pacific International Exposition

San Francisco, California 1915

I did indeed find the map to the Exposition carefully set in my grandmother's scrapbook. The map was folded but very much intact, even though by the time I came across it in 1960, it had been 45 years since my grandparents attended this important worldwide event. For the city of San Francisco, the Exposition celebrated its re-emergence after the earthquake and fire, while the world celebrated the opening of the Panama Canal for ships of commerce and travelers alike. These two events ushered in the twentieth century for much of the world. One of the posters for the Exposition showed Hercules pushing two continents apart, representing the builders of the canal.

Vintage postcard welcoming visitors to Panama-Pacific Exposition in San Francisco, 1915 (PPIE 100.org)

Lottie and Philip Lynch
~1915~

Lottie and Phil spent several days that sometimes stretched into the evenings at the Panama-Pacific International Exposition that year. They had never seen such sights: palaces showing exhibits from each of the states, food demonstrations, spectacular, oversized machinery. The grand fair covered 635 acres stretching over two miles of reclaimed marshland on the bay side of San Francisco. There were more than 80,000 exhibits—so much to see and do! The fair took seven years from planning to reality. In those years, San Francisco had risen up like the phoenix from the '06 earthquake and fire to rebuild itself completely.

By the time the Exposition opened its gates on February 20, 1915, the City had been resettled and business was humming along. It was a new century and there were amazing inventions to showcase: aviation, instant long-distance communication, diesel power. There were airplane rides to be taken over the bay. Phil gladly paid $10 for his very first airplane ride.

"Business is good now," he said to Lottie. "I have the cash in my pocket. Mother, let's try it. I want to see what it's like to fly."

"I don't know." Lottie shook her head. "You go on, if you must. I'll wait here, just in case." At this point in her young life, she'd seen enough troubles. At times the train wreck in 1903 still flashed in her mind, even though it was a full twelve years ago. And the shaking and aftershocks of the '06 quake had left her with another layer of hesitancy. Yet she was the one who, when elected May Queen at age eleven, had promised her subjects on Grand Island that she "would get them each an airplane."

"I'll be fine," Phil assured her. He looked admiringly at the two-seater Model G Hydro-plane. He willingly signed the waiver that assumed he was responsible for "all risks of any nature." The pilot helped him adjust his goggles while Phil tightened his jacket around him, thinking that even though it was spring, the air could be cold up there.

"I'm off into the wild blue yonder," he said to no one at all as he stepped onto the small plane. He was astounded when the propeller whirred as the engine started up. The plane rose from the water next to the Yacht Harbor and flew up into the air so smoothly that Philip was aloft in no time, peering over the sides of his seat high above the Presidio, over the Golden Gate to the Marin Headlands, back to Sausalito, and over the small island of Alcatraz. In the ten-minute ride he felt the rush of flying wind in his hair, only peeking down between the floorboards once for a quick glimpse of the blue waters of the bay below.

"Oh, Phil!" Lottie ran to meet him after he safely landed. "How was it? Were you scared? What did you see?"

"It was grand, Mother! Felt just like a bird. I saw everything from Marin County to Mt. Diablo. I hope this flying catches on, people will be able to go anywhere. Maybe our own kids will fly over the sea to Europe, or our great-grandchildren will fly to Panama, or even Africa."

Panama-Pacific Exposition aerial view, 1915 (Wikimedia Commons)

Lottie just sighed. Perhaps Phil was right about travel, but she preferred to stay right here in the Bay Area and to travel by paddlewheel steamer to the Delta to see her family. That's all the travel she ever wanted now. She'd had enough of risks in her life already, but she knew that with men and boys you have to just let them get things out of their systems. She took this attitude when she dared look up at her husband in the air over the Bay and hoped for the best.

"Let's take the Overfair Railway to the next exhibition, and we'll get a bite to eat on the way," Lottie suggested.

"That's fine with me," Phil said. "On the way back, I'd like to rent one of those wicker basket electric cars. I think they're called "Electriquettes." I'll drive. It will be easier than a team of horses. They're like automobiles, but don't use gas—maybe the auto industry will take to them."

On their way they stopped at the Exposition's Palace of Food Products and happily sampled Alaskan salmon, Japanese tea, Chinese almond cakes, Mexican tamales, and Russian *piroshkis*. They stared in awe at the 11,000-pound Big Cheese sent in from New York—the largest cheese ever made! The American Chicle Company exhibit was also something to see, explaining how gum was made.

"Electriquette" battery-powered electric car
(*Edison Monthly*, Vol 9, 1916)

Lottie was fascinated by the canning demonstrations. She was glad to see that the manufacturers of food were finally able to can fruits and vegetables in a sanitary and safe manner. She had spent so many summers putting food by and canning her own family's foods that the convenience of buying some canned goods at the market was a relief.

Phil had been a farmer when he was a boy and took in the latest ideas from the Palace of Agriculture. The animated diorama of four seasons on a model farm caught his eye. The exhibit insisted that engines would take the place of manpower, and that was grand to him. He recalled many years of driving his dad's team of twenty horses under the hot Brentwood sun, plus milking the cows in the early morning. Now he saw models of a gasoline engine providing power to the farm's lights, milk house and machinery. The farming machine exhibit by International Harvester showed many tasks formerly done by manpower humming along with ease—powered by the new gasoline engines.

"I think if I ever had to go back to farming, Lottie, I'd hope to get these machines to do the work for me."

"Let's hope you never have to go back to the farm, Phil. You know how much I love the City, and now that we're in Burlingame we've got the best of both worlds."

After sampling the food court and the Palace of Agriculture, the last stop they would make was to the Palace of Manufacturers and Industries. Lottie was delighted to see the Home Electrical exhibition, which included electric fireplaces, player pianos, toasters and coffeemakers. They were all running on their own. The only human intervention needed was the flick of a switch!

"Imagine that!" she said to Phil. "I wouldn't have to use my feet to run the sewing machine. But I guess it will be a while before we get a new sewing machine, right?"

"Well, give these inventions a few years to straighten themselves out and get them working all right, and then electricity will pan out. What do you think of this electric stove, Mother?"

"I'm not sure. How would I regulate the temperature? I'll wait on that one. Oh look, there's a whole group of folks sewing children's overalls in the Levi Strauss area. Now, there's a good use for electricity!"

It would take Lottie and Phil several more days over the course of that spring and summer to see the rest of the fair. Lottie spied a beautiful fish platter, handmade in Germany, that her aunt Cecelia gave to her later that year.

There were the new modern record players and the first colored photography they ever saw. You could even talk on telephone lines that travelled on wires, coast to coast. Some folks were even talking to Hawaii! At times, all these new inventions and electric machines took a while to get used to. But the possibility of saving one's back and putting manual labor behind was a welcome reality.

On one of their visits they witnessed a full assembly line of the Model T Ford automobile. It produced eighteen complete cars every afternoon from 2 to 5 pm, or one about every 10 minutes. Phil watched in wonder. He worked five days a week in the City at his fuel yard, supplying the city's houses with coal and their horses with hay and grain. He could see that the hay and grain already weren't needed as much. There was no way around it; the automobile was coming in. So many folks could buy one now, and they were giving up horses in favor of this noisier, oil-eating way to travel. Phil wondered how folks could afford the $500 price tag on a Dodge, or the Ford Model T at $750. Why, even the gasoline was expensive at 10 cents a gallon!

But these days, autos were getting folks around town, and going further than the trains could take them out of town. The demand was beginning for new paved roads, smooth roads that wouldn't blow out an automobile's rubber tires. Now, with a team of horses that was never a problem. But progress was happening. As he watched those autos flow off the assembly line at the Exposition, his mind was working on ways to find new markets for coal in more homes and businesses. The Diablo Coal Mine in the East Bay still produced plenty of fuel, a basic need for heating and cooking, which he delivered to homes and businesses in the City. But it was a new century, and his work providing hay and grain for horses, he could see, would gradually come to an end. And it was fabulous, really, how smooth and fast the automobiles ran. He'd like to have one himself one day.

At the end of their visits to the Exposition, Lottie and Phil drove their horse and buggy up and over the hills of San Francisco. They could see the lights glowing all over the fairgrounds into the City from the "Tower of Jewels," lit up at night and casting rainbows of color over San Francisco. This was due, once again, to the marvel of electricity. It was a sight they would never forget.

Many nights as they lay in their bed in Burlingame, the children already sound asleep, the couple was satisfied with the life they had built together. They looked forward to the future in this new century with its electric inventions to make life easier, the automobile to take you anywhere you wanted to go, and plenty of food on their table. It seemed they had it all. By the time the Panama-Pacific International Exposition closed in December of 1915, the whole Bay Area was full of pride and happy in its return to the world stage once again.

Souvenir booklet showing lights from the Tower of Jewels,
Panama-Pacific Exposition, 1915 (Wikimedia Commons)

CHAPTER 14
George Russell Lynch
December 1915

Camilla, Walter, and Jack Lynch, three of Charlotte & Phil's
six young children (Author Collection)

Life in the Lynch household in the Panama-Pacific Exposition year of 1915, with five sons and one daughter, was busy and full, to say the least. Walter, their oldest son at age eleven, was studious and somewhat serious. Phil Jr., age eight, was in third grade. He loved stories and always had a joke to tell. Camilla, six years old at the time, was a good student who loved giving pretend tea parties and dressing up. At four years old, Donald was about ready to start kindergarten. Jack, now almost three years old, followed his big brothers everywhere and loved to climb trees.

Russell, age one-and-a-half, was their baby, beloved by all. He was redheaded like his mother and siblings Phil Jr. and Camilla. Russell was the apple of his family's eyes. Nearly ready to form words, he babbled all the time in a language all his own, and the children knew what he wanted. They were glad to give him pony rides on their big dog's back, carry him around, and play with him and his fire truck when he needed attention. When Philip Sr. came home from work, Russell was often the first to greet his dad at the door, where he would be willingly scooped up in Phil's arms and carried into the kitchen.

We all knew, my eleven cousins and I, that we had another uncle, Russell, but he does not stand in the 1953 photo of my grandparents' fiftieth wedding anniversary at the Sheraton Palace Hotel. This is the photo we all hold so dear. In this photo you see my grandparents, Charlotte and Philip. Surrounding them are six of their seven children and their families: Walter, Philip Jr., Camilla, Donald D, Jack, and Barbara. Russell is the seventh child, always counted in by each one. Russell is one that they all missed.

The Worst Month
~December, 1915~

The past six weeks had been unbearably long and arduous. The family had such a shock when the doctor ordered, "Quarantine the house! It's scarlet fever. The four boys have contracted it, the girl has not, and Russell's not showing signs yet. Watch them all. The baby's at the most risk."

They had their job ahead of them, taking care of six children, with Philip worrying about the family and wondering constantly how his business in the City was faring. With the quarantine in place, there was no way Philip could leave his home for at least six weeks, so he had no way to answer any of these questions. Thank goodness for the meals that were left on the front porch by kindly neighbors.

There were round-the-clock nurses whose shifts changed every eight hours. Philip had to hire and pay them every two weeks, as well as pay the doctor for his visits and consultations. They had no medical insurance, which wasn't yet offered to individuals at the time. Lottie and Philip did what they could to keep the recovering children busy with coloring books, games of Tiddlywinks and platoons of small toy soldiers. The whole family could not go outside in the street. And there were the reminders on the radio that Christmas was coming soon, but they could not go to the store to buy gifts.

QUARANTINE
SCARLET FEVER

All persons are forbidden to enter or leave these premises without the permission of the HEALTH OFFICER under PENALTY OF THE LAW.

Quarantine scarlet fever poster, circa 1910 (US National Library of Medicine)

Their meat and vegetables were delivered; however, the milkman couldn't come around as he used to, because he was forbidden to touch any bottles that might be infected. Everyone knew you could get scarlet fever from just breathing the air next to a sick person, and you couldn't touch anything that the sick person had used until the doctor declared the house germ free. Neighbors could not visit; even George Douglas, their good friend right next door, could not drop by like he usually did. Philip and Lottie would talk by telephone to family and friends, and the radio was a steady source of news of the outside world. There were times when they both reassured themselves with thoughts that the world was indeed continuing, and with hopes that they would rejoin the pace of life soon. This consoled them and let them march on.

The older boys began to recover at four weeks into the siege, but Russell showed signs of illness and was too young to fight it off. They all stayed indoors from the first of November until late December 1915. The house on Acacia Avenue in Burlingame was big enough, with four bedrooms, a grand kitchen and a parlor, but it couldn't contain the rampage of this illness. The worry

FDA warning to milk truckers, circa early 1900s (Library of Congress)

over everyone's health left Philip and Lottie with many sleepless nights and frayed nerves during the days. When the baby began to worsen, their sadness wouldn't quit.

After all, Russell was the one all the siblings played with. Before this time, when everyone was well, his two oldest brothers, Walter and Philip, used to toss him in the air and catch him with ease, as Russell's high-pitched squeals delighted everyone.

"Now you two be careful with the baby," Lottie would scold, to no avail. She knew by now that life with five boys was both energetic and surprising.

"We're careful, Mother, don't worry!" they would shout above the din of the family escapades.

Camilla loved Russell as only a six-year-old big sister could. "Can I let the baby come to my tea party, Mama?" she would beg.

"Yes dear, but only one cookie! And let Donald and Jack have one too."

"Oh Mama, Don and Jack get into everything and wreck it," Camilla retorted. Camilla learned to close the door to her room, locking Don and Jack outside while they happily munched on stolen treats. She let Russell stay with her. She dressed him up in fancy clothes and tried to get him to stop wiggling and sit down while she poured the tea. Camilla also loved the game where all the youngest siblings took turns riding on the back of their big spaniel, Freckles. Last spring Camilla was the one who told Don and Jack to make sure Russell held on tight to Freckles' shaggy mane as both dog and rider loped around the wide-open spaces of their Burlingame backyard.

But this past month there was no more riding nor much fun to be had, with almost everyone in their household affected by the ravages of the fever. Lottie and Phil Sr. did not contract the disease; Walt and Philip Jr. got through it fastest, and Don and Jack were slower to recover but on the mend by early December. But the baby could not shake it. The doctor confirmed on his visit that if Russell's fever wouldn't go down, he was in trouble. They tried everything: cool sponge baths for the fever, then tight wraps for chills. He began to lose weight and wouldn't eat. All the effort and love of those last weeks and days could not help. On December 19, 1915, Little Russell's fate sent him to an early death. He is the brother who would live on in all the family's hearts forever.

When Russell died at just twenty-one months of age, Lottie's heart sank deeper than she ever thought it could.

Oh, how to bear up after these six long weeks, nursing her sick children, hoping for health of all of them, then losing the baby? Hope after hope was gone now, and Russell would never become a little boy. He lay still in her arms with no warmth anymore about him. Lottie had wrapped him up so often this year; now she just held him there and sank into Philip's arms. Philip's arms—the arms that could always make everything better. She could hear her husband's heart beat so sad and slow with each breath. Both of them realized now that they had life, something they could not will back into their baby.

Yet Russell needed tending now, even still. Tears moved in rivers along her cheeks as Lottie unwrapped Russell and bathed his small body with warm water. Her hands gently washed his curly red locks as they had hundreds of times before. She dried him all over, dressed him in his little sailor suit, folded his arms across his body, and with her fingertips she gently closed his eyes. She brushed his beautiful hair, and said to Philip, "Now you may make the call." This was the moment he had dreaded over the past six weeks—a call to the coroner's office. Philip had never wanted to make this call for any of his children.

Two days after Russell's death, there was the inconsolable sorrow of his funeral and burial at Holy Cross Cemetery, where Philip and Lottie and the family said goodbye to their youngest boy. Philip silently witnessed Lottie place the metal toy fire truck beside the baby's small coffin. He gathered his children around him and shepherded his wife back home.

The grief was felt all through the neighborhood. Their neighbor George Douglas published this poignant eulogy for little Russell:

"The thought of the millions mercilessly slaughtered on the battle fields of Europe has many and many a time depressed us, and yet the deepest grief we have known in years came on Sunday afternoon when the death angel paid a sudden visit next door and left us minus the spirit of the little boy who had barely learned to lisp our name. We talk of death in millions, but we can only feel it through an individual touch."

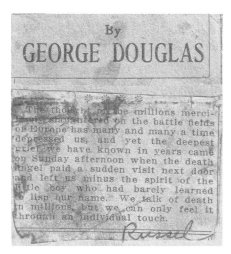

Eulogy for Russell by George Douglas,
journalist, Lynch neighbor and friend,
San Francisco Chronicle, circa April
1915 (Author Collection)

Quarantine was not unusual in 1915. When a disease such as scarlet fever spread through towns and neighborhoods, it was sadly common to see a red sign on the door declaring in bold letters: "Quarantine Scarlet Fever–All persons are forbidden to enter or leave these premises without the permission of the Health Officer Under Penalty of the Law." Other notices decreed, "No Person shall be allowed to enter, lease or take any article from this house without written permission by a legalized agent of the Board of Health, excepting physicians, nurses in charge of the sick or clergymen. Animals may not be permitted to leave these premises."

Although scarlet fever was once a serious childhood illness, antibiotic treatments, first available in the early 1940s, have made it less threatening. Today, outcomes with scarlet fever are typically good. But it was a leading cause of death in children in the early twentieth century.

"Oh, my brothers were affected," my mother Barbara told me. "Phil Jr. had a goiter in his throat, and Don had a bad ear for the rest of his life."

She went on to explain about her youngest brother Jack, the sibling she felt closest to. "Well," she said, "before the scarlet fever, Jack was as quick as the rest of them, sharp, you know. But after that, my sister and brothers will tell you, Jack was a bit slower than he had been. That time affected my whole family, but my mother never quite got over the death of Russell."

Barbara sighed and looked out the window. "There was a time when one of our extended family members passed away suddenly, maybe six or seven years after Russell died. The family didn't have another burial plot, and they asked if they could use the same gravesite where Russell was buried. My mother had to agree to dig up her son's grave to make room for the other one. She told me that she was so upset about it all. She went to Russell's gravesite on the day his coffin was exhumed, because she wanted to make sure that Russell's fire truck would still be buried next to him. She made sure that it was. I believe in my heart that Russell's little fire truck is there to this day."

PART FOUR
Farm and City Life
1916–1955

CHAPTER 15
Dust and Hope
Life on the Brentwood Farm
1916–1921

Russell's death and the quarantine turned my grandparents' family tide in a direction that no one could have foreseen. Before that terrible year, though Philip could see changes coming with the automobile, my grandfather's business was thriving. Most ordinary folks still used the horse and buggy, and all the grain needed to feed these necessary animals was grown by farms outside the City. Almost everyone needed coal for heat. He sold and delivered grain and coal to households and merchants in downtown San Francisco. Business was so good that my grandfather hired a partner, Mr. Hennessey, to keep the books and watch over the cash for the thriving yard on Sutter Street.

But the quarantine knocked the stability of this life on its head. My grandfather couldn't go to work for weeks. The doctor's and nurses' bills mounted as the weeks dragged by. Philip hoped he had enough cash in the business to pay them. Then the final blow struck. A few days after Russell's funeral service, when Phil felt that Charlotte could manage and the children were somewhat recovered, he returned to the yard on Sutter. There he discovered that Hennessey had robbed him of almost every dime! His partner had taken advantage of his six-week absence and had been taking from the till.

He left only the horses and a few sacks of coal and bales of hay. Philip's cash reserves had all been spent on costs from scarlet fever. It not only had taken his baby, but now also his livelihood and his ability to continue with business as usual. Hennessey skipped town, never to be heard from again.

Philip and Lottie Lynch
~1916~

After living through these last two hardest months of his life, Philip summoned all the willpower he had. He grew determined to survive—somehow—both the crushing blows of Russell's death and the loss of his business. With no cash reserves to buy new supplies, his business was all but finished.

Over the next six months into 1916, he formed a plan in his mind that he thought might work. He could go back to farming the East Bay homestead in Brentwood where he'd grown up. On the farm, he'd had eighteen years of planting, tilling, and harvesting on his father's 1,000 acres, enough to know farming in his bones. Going back to farming was his last good option. He still had five kids and a wife to support, and he felt that farm life would be good for the boys. Perhaps Lottie would recover better in the country air as well. Of course, since he was the oldest boy in his family with eight younger brothers on the farm, Philip knew the hard work and discipline that his growing sons would need to learn to become real helpers on the farm.

They needed a fresh start in a new place. Besides, truth be told, he'd had enough of the hustle and bustle of the City. He did not have the means to start another hay, grain and coal business, and he didn't have experience with selling automobiles or gasoline. Philip had a feeling that the country might enter another a war, if what he'd read in the daily papers was any indication. Already, Germany, England and France had declared war on one another. If the United States entered the war, he knew that he could grow wheat and barley for the soldiers. His plan was to lease back the 100 acres of farmland he had sold to his mother when he first left home. He could bring the family back to his boyhood land in the small East Bay town of Brentwood. He hoped constantly that Lottie would recover from the shock of Russell's death, and that they all would get a new lease on life after this terrible and sorrow-filled time.

A few months after Russell's death they packed up, sold some of the furniture, and kept what they could of Lottie's fine china and silver. They made the arrangements with Philip's mother for the farmland in Brentwood, within the shadow of Mount Diablo. Philip vowed to himself with God as his witness that they would get past the shadow of scarlet fever for another try at life.

The family's ferry ride over the Bay to the Oakland train station in spring of 1916 was filled with sadness and hope. Just months ago, he had everything. Now he was minus one son, his business was gone, and a new livelihood of farming was to begin. Having moved to San Francisco at eighteen, he'd been away from it from it for almost twenty years. He prayed this solution would be the one that would pan out. Though he thought his boys would do well with life on the farm, he was not sure at all about Lottie or his daughter Camilla.

On the train from Oakland to Antioch, three of the boys, Phil, Don and Jack, kept running up and down the aisles. Lottie and Camilla sat quietly next to Phil. Walt tried to corral his younger brothers into doing anything except getting into mischief.

As they traveled that day, Lottie's brain could not comprehend how her life had turned upside down this time. Her heart was empty, just when it had been so full. She stared out the window at land she knew well from

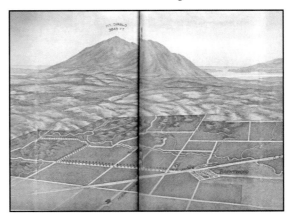

The small town of Brentwood, lower right in vast farmlands of Diablo Valley, circa 1930 (J. Loomis, *Brentwood: Images of America*, 2008)

childhood. But this side of the Sacramento Delta near Mt. Diablo was so dry, even now in late June. Lottie saw nothing but sadness in the brown and somewhat still-green soft hills of the East Bay. She thought, *There's nothing but hard work ahead.* She knew she might not see those days again when she could hire help, someone to do the washing and ironing. She had seen the farm, the place they would lease back from Phil's mother Ellen. It was primitive, with only an outhouse. Even though Lottie was always happy cooking, now she would be expected to do it all: cook, clean, wash and iron, mend. Camilla was only seven, a willing child, off to herself most times, and too young to be of real help. The rest were boys, expected to help with the farm, but not with women's work.

Lottie looked up into the cloudless sky and prayed. She prayed for help, prayed for this heartache to ease so she could raise her four boys and one daughter on the farm at the crossing of Deer Valley Road and Lone Tree Way.

Soon enough she got to know the day-to-day life of Brentwood. Their new home was shocking when they arrived: a plain wooden structure with two bedrooms, a living room, dining room, kitchen, and the outhouse. She had used outdoor privies on the Delta as a child, but Lord, when she moved to San Francisco fifteen years before, she thought those days were over! And there was the constant heat. The family was now relocated only thirty miles as the crow flies from the cool afternoon breezes of her childhood home in Isleton, by the Delta's fresh river waters. But what a difference those thirty miles made! Brentwood was dusty, hot, dry, and overshadowed by the devil's mountain, Mount Diablo. There was always the heat and the lack of fresh water. The well water in Brentwood was alkaline and bitter, not fit to drink nor to cook with. Philip and Charlotte rented a water wagon like all the other farm families, and hauled 1,000 gallons of fresh water to fill the cement cistern out back of the house every six weeks. Brentwood's rolling hills looked refreshing in the spring, green and inviting. Then spring gave way to summer and fall, when the dust began to settle in.

All the family relied on Lottie's cooking, and she found some solace there. But the rest of farm life—why, she hated it. Hated the way the heat seared the dust into your clothes and hair, and the constant gathering of wood from the woodpile for baths, the stove, the wash. The animals were around all the time, the chickens needed to be fed, the cow milked. She did get one of those new wringer washing machines, which made doing five loads a week somewhat easier. The ironing took up most of her afternoons. All the physical work made her stronger, yes, but at the end of each day, she was so tired.

In reality, Philip endured Brentwood as much as Lottie did, witnessing her unhappiness, sharing her grief over Russell's death, day to day, month to month, year to year. But he kept hoping this move would get them back on their feet, financially able to live comfortably once again. Lottie cooked and cleaned, and Phil knew boys, their energy, their natural bent towards mischief. Mostly he put them to work.

The two oldest—Walt just twelve, and Phil Jr. almost ten years old—were just about the age he had been when his dad had put him to work on the big jobs. Just like his dad had taught him, Phil showed Walt and Phil Jr. how to hitch up and drive the teams of horses for planting the wheat and barley. The country had in fact gone to war, and Phil knew those

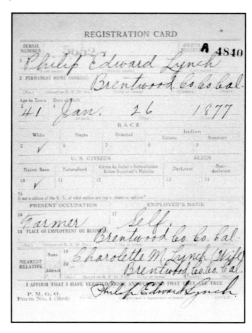

Philip Edward Lynch draft card, 1917
(Author Collection)

crops were the surest bets for the government to buy to feed the soldiers. He did have to register for the draft in 1917 at the age of forty-one, but was granted a deferment due to his large family and his age.

Philip counted on what his dad had taught him about farming: hitch the teams, plant the seeds in winter, tend in summer, and plow in the fall. "Pray for rain, son," his dad would tell him in his Irish brogue, "Pray for rain." And in those years of Philip's youth the rains fell steady and reliably, the crops got planted and he and his brothers and sisters slept well in the family's first farmhouse high up on the hill.

In Philip's heart, he planted seeds and prayed for rain while the boys and Camilla went to school, learning their ABCs and sums in the one-room Lone Tree Schoolhouse. Their teacher, Miss Violet Trembath, kept them all in order until the three o'clock bell when they were set free. Three of the Lynch boys rode on horseback to the grammar school along the mile-long dirt road. Camilla had to ride with the loser of the straw vote, as they had to go slower with her eight-year-old self in the back of the saddle. The Lynches were smart kids and did well in school.

After school, they'd go straight home and Lottie would have cookies, cake or pies waiting for them. Camilla helped Lottie in the house and the boys worked after school and

Wheat harvester with twenty mules, Brentwood, circa early 1900s
(Carol A. Jensen, *Brentwood: Images of America,* 2008)

Lone Tree School, with students from local families: Lynch, Williamson, McFar-
lan, Gann, Golden, and Loryea, 1896 (Antioch Historical Society,
Images of America: Antioch, 2005)

in summer on the farm. Though their chores kept them busy, Phil, Don, and Walt had free time for mischief between jobs and on weekends. One afternoon as Jack and Don rode home from school, they got hungry, as growing boys will. They saw bunches of grapes ripe and juicy, waiting just for them that late September. They figured nobody was around, got out of the wagon, picked bunches of grapes and began to gobble them up. Suddenly they were startled by gunshots.

"Get off my land, you thieves!" Farmer Pruitt shouted. The boys rushed to the wagon, dropping all the grapes and barely catching up with the spooked horse. They hightailed it towards the house, hoping their dad wouldn't find out, but in a small town of only forty families, everyone knew everyone else and they caught it when they got home.

When Don was seven, he had a penchant for sneaking out instead of doing his homework, crawling underneath the fences to see friends or wander about. His dad outfoxed him several times by figuring out his escape routes and tying dead snakes to the fence posts. This deterred his young son most of the time.

"Oh, Mother never got over Brentwood," every last one of her children would reflect throughout their lives, as they recalled the hard work on the farm that required Lottie to be up at dawn, stoking the fire in the woodstove to cook breakfast for their family of eight, and at harvest times for several hired ranch hands. Camilla and Jack remembered getting up after the rooster crowed to gather eggs before school, while Phil and Don helped their dad hitch up the teams for plowing. Lottie slowly recovered, raising her sons and Camilla, and bore her last child, my mother Barbara. Despite the shock of finding herself in a hardworking farming life, my grandmother persevered.

Barbara Mahoney with brother Phil Lynch in Brentwood, 1992. They grew up in the small farmhouse shown in background, where their parents Lottie and Philip moved in 1916 (Author Collection)

CHAPTER 16

Lynch's Wild West Rodeo Show

Brentwood 1919
Walter, Phil, Camilla, Don and Jack Lynch

A favorite family story is about one of the greatest times my uncles and aunt had, staging a self-made rodeo. Philip and Lottie decided that Walter was old enough at 15 to watch over their brood while they went off to the real rodeo in Antioch. Phil Jr., age 12, Donald, age 8, and Jack, age 6, were left blissfully alone with only their oldest brother Walter and Camilla, the wise 10-year-old sister, to try to rein them in.

"Let's have our own rodeo, right here in our corral!" Phil Jr. suggested when his parents were out of sight.

"Yeah, that's a swell idea," Don chimed in. "I'll be the bucking bronco rider!"

"No," Walter explained calmly. "I will be the rodeo master and you three will be the cowboys. We'll have horse races and roping. It'll be swell." At this point Walt couldn't see any harm in this idea; after all, they had been living on the farm for three years already, and the kids knew the animals well. "Let's get going."

"What'll *I* do, Walt?" asked six-year-old young Jack.

"Well, we'll figure that out later," said Walt. "Meanwhile, Jack, you and Don get the ropes out and start practicing. Phil and I will get the horses saddled up."

Don chimed in, "Jack and I can do tricks with the dogs. Maybe we could light a hoop on fire so the dogs can go through."

"Now, wait a minute. No fire!" demanded Camilla, who was listening carefully to the whole plan. She was the third oldest, and as she'd gotten into trouble the least amount of times, her point of view did carry some weight. "You remember what happened when Don and Jack set that fire near the creek and our dog Shep was tied to the post last summer? We *all* caught it from Dad that time. No fires."

"Absolutely no fire." Walt glared at his three younger brothers. "I'm the rodeo master, and this whole show nobody gets in trouble. Nothing stupid, got it?" Don, Phil and Jack solemnly nodded their heads.

Camilla pointed at her brothers. "That's right. No fires, but I'll take the tickets. I think the neighbors will want to come." She fluffed up her red curls. "I'll wear my new boots and sparkly shirt and ride around the corral on Daisy's back. She is the prettiest horse, and tame. You boys can put on kerchiefs like real cowboys and comb your hair, even Jack. What shall we call ourselves?"

"The Lynch's Wild West Rodeo Show! Today only, 2 cents admission," Phil commanded. "Camilla, take Jack around to the Williamson's place, Pruitt's, the Cakebreads and Shallenbergers. Those kids will all come."

Camilla chimed in, "We can't let them have any food, Mom will notice."

"Aw, no food, no fair!" countered the younger boys.

"No food! This will be after lunch anyway, and we'll have to make everything right in the corral by nightfall when Mom and Dad come home. Everything will be back to normal."

This merry band of brothers and one sister spent the morning getting the various animals into the main part of the corral. The sheep were easy and the ram they dragged with a rope. The baby calf mooed loudly, as she was only four months old. Camilla brought in Daisy by her halter, and by the time she got her hair combed and tied a bandanna around her own neck, they were set for the show to begin.

Everything went off as planned, or unplanned. The rope shows got a lot of applause from the neighborhood kids. At that time Phil could swing ropes round his head, and he helped Walt tie the calf up. Jack and Don had the dogs do several great tricks that involved fetching and jumping through fireless hoops. The last two events were great in theory but just didn't work out as planned.

Because young Jack was so little and fearless, the boys decided he would be the one to jump out of the top of the hayloft onto a rodeo animal's back and take off, just like they'd seen in the silent movies in the nearby town. "Yeah, I can do it," said Jack. "I'll whistle when I'm all set, you whistle back, then I'll jump away. Which horse will it be?"

"Not Daisy!" shouted Camilla.

Walt suggested the new calf. "She's still young and won't run too fast."

"Okay. I'll be up waiting till you whistle when she's ready."

Jack clambered up the ladder, and Walt announced the next act. Phil and Don got the baby calf and held her still, then placed her in what they thought was just the right spot. Walt whistled, Jack jumped with great joy, and landed square on the poor little calf's back. She was so startled by this arrival from above that she couldn't get her bearings, panicked and fell to the ground, then got up, hobbling on all fours. Jack was fine, he jumped right up, but Walt cautioned, "Don't get back on her, Jack. She needs to get un-dizzy."

There was a little pause in the action, with one final act still to go. The siblings, in all their cumulative wisdom, couldn't foresee the outcome of this daredevil act either. Walt and Phil thought the final act should be the most dramatic, so they decided that Don would be the star, because he was the biggest one of them at the time.

"Don," said Phil, "You're the last and most exciting act."

"What is it?"

"I've seen it lots of times at the real rodeo over in Antioch," said Phil Jr. "It's called the Ram Run."

"I don't know," Don said hesitantly.

"No, go on, it'll be fine," assured Phil. "We'll tie a big pillow to you, and you'll be tied up to the post over there. The ram will softly butt the pillow, that's all. It's the grand finale!"

"Are you sure, fellas? I don't want to get hurt or nothin'!" Don said skeptically.

Walt announced the grand finale, and then…

The ram ran straight into Don. The pillow was hardly a help. Don ended up with several of his ribs out of place. He was really banged up, but he never told his parents that he was hurting with each breath he took. His mom asked him that night and several days later why he was grunting every time he took a breath. He said nothing and neither did the others. When Phil and Lottie surmised what had happened, they all caught hell for the rodeo, even Camilla. The calf's back was broken, and she was never right since. For that they were all truly sorry. They hadn't meant to hurt the animals at all. Phil Senior and Lottie punished them all with extra chores, made them come right home after school, and the boys were kept busier than ever from sunup to sundown on the ranch. Camilla had to clean her brother's shirts with bluing that summer and fall. She regretted having a bunch of brothers ever since.

Seventy years later, Uncle Don recalled the rodeo with a glint of mischief in his eyes. "Oh yeah, one day in the corral, we did have our own rodeo. We rode cows, calves and sheep, and we had a hell of a time! Phil tells quite a story about me riding a bighorn sheep but that wasn't true; he made that up. Of course, we did break the back of one of the calves and we were sorry for that. I remember my brothers and I slept in a tent underneath the eucalyptus tree in the summers. It was great living on the farm."

However, when asked about it, my mother Barbara shook her head. "My brothers were a wild bunch. My dad had to keep them in line all the time. I wasn't born yet when they had the rodeo. Thank God. It's a wonder I ever got married at all, what with all those boys and their mischief. I remember they'd be play shooting at the dinner table, and later they were bringing home ducks for Mother to clean, the feathers were all over the bathtub. They'd swing golf clubs all around the house. I don't know how I survived!" She told me this over lunch, rolling her eyes, settling her then-ninety-four years into the matriarch's chair at the head of our family table. She spoke in her usual calm manner, with a touch of wry humor thrown in. Maybe that is how she survived.

CHAPTER 17
Lottie Employs Her Talents

In the years after the death of her beloved Russell, by the light of the gas lanterns on the Brentwood farm, my grandmother Lottie slowly got herself back. She nourished herself back to life. Even though she now saw the world through heartbroken eyes, her talent for elocution and love of the theater gave her solace and an escape from farm life. As with so many who came before and after, Lottie found ways to keep her spirits steady during the years on the farm by joining others who gathered together in small California communities to put on plays, give lectures, and hold music recitals.

The local newspaper reviews of Lottie's theater and elocution performances are impressive. She cut them out and pasted them into her scrapbook.

February 21, 1917 Mrs. Philip Lynch favored us with a reading entitled "The Diver" which demonstrated she possessed ability above and beyond the ordinary and she will no doubt be called upon to appear on many occasions. Mrs. Lynch but recently removed from San Francisco to this place and was very popular in Bay City social circles where she took part in many affairs.

May 28, 1918 *Large Attendance At Catholic Entertainment*

Mrs. P. E. Lynch gave two recitations, the first being of a serious nature, but well interpreted, while the latter was humorous. Both were well received…

April 15, 1921 "All of a Sudden Peggy," which was staged at the Auditorium Friday by the Parent-Teachers association was a success far beyond their expectations. At an early hour, every seat in the house with many extra seats in the aisles were filled and a number were standing…Peggy was adorable in her part of the lassie, impulsive, and sudden to a degree, getting her into scrapes, the consequences of which she only escaped from by her loveableness. Mrs. Phil Lynch portrayed this star part in a manner to discount several professionals.

For most of her thirties, Lottie worked hard on the farm. In July 1919 she had her last child, my mother Barbara. Still, with six children, and after an unbearable tragedy, she continued to fulfill her calling to perform on the stage, the dream that had brought her to San Francisco all those years before. She practiced her lines long into the evenings. She drove herself to rehearsals in the family's brassbound Ford with isinglass windows. Philip stayed home with their brood of four boys and now two girls, giving infant Barbara her bottles during those long nights.

Newspaper clipping, *Brentwood Times,* noting Mrs. Phil Lynch starring role
(Charlotte's scrapbook, Author Collection)

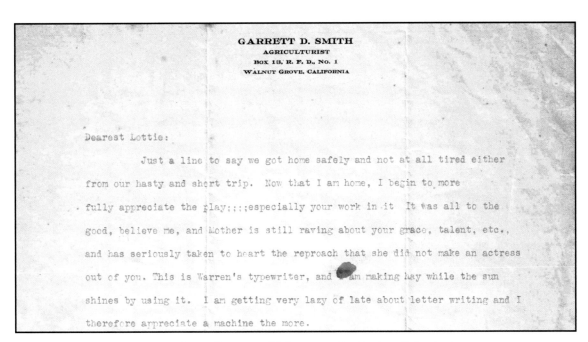

GARRETT D. SMITH
AGRICULTURIST
BOX 13, R. F. D., No. 1
WALNUT GROVE, CALIFORNIA

Dearest Lottie:

Just a line to say we got home safely and not at all tired either
from our hasty and short trip. Now that I am home, I begin to more
fully appreciate the play;;;;especially your work in it It was all to the
good, believe me, and Mother is still raving about your grace, talent, etc.,
and has seriously taken to heart the reproach that she did not make an actress
out of you. This is Warren's typewriter, and I am making hay while the sun
shines by using it. I am getting very lazy of late about letter writing and I
therefore appreciate a machine the more.

Letter to Lottie from sister Veda, circa 1921 (Author Collection)

Along with newspaper clippings, Lottie saved a letter from her sister Veda, written on her father Garrett Smith's letterhead. Veda had traveled from Walnut Grove to Brentwood with their mother Marie Louise, then in her early sixties, to see Lottie in a play.

"Dearest Lottie," Veda wrote after their trip, "Now that I am home, I begin to more fully appreciate the play, especially your work in it. It was all to the good, believe me, and Mother is still raving about your grace, talent, etc., and has seriously taken to heart the reproach that she did not make an actress out of you…"

Veda, who was single at the time, was also moved by Lottie's full family life. "Believe me, Lottie," she continued, "you have a wonderful family. They are all so interesting and busy. It was a regular revelation to me to see them enjoying their work. They are dear kids, every one of them and believe me, they interest me and I can't forget them. The ranch has made men and women (Barbie can hardly be classed as a woman yet, but Camilla has all the makin's) out of them. You can't see this because you are with them all the time…Believe me I am glad you both are not spoiling them!"

My grandmother's scrapbook also documents her enjoyment of country balls and dances. Dances such as the waltz, foxtrot, and one-step were popular dances at the time. In the early 1900s, custom dictated that men sign for dances with potential partners on the woman's dance card. Lottie pasted a dance card from the Farm Center's Second Annual Ball on May 21, 1921 in her scrapbook.

Still, even after all their plans and hard work, Phil and Lottie saw their funds dwindling. After two successful years farming, there had been no rain in their dry fields for the last three years. The worst drought to date in California's history came and stayed. Unfortunately, by late 1921, their family was close to bankruptcy once again. There was not enough cash to pay for farm supplies for the next year.

By then, all of her children will tell you, Lottie declared herself *through*! She fingered her wedding ring as she began to hatch a plan for a future back in San Francisco.

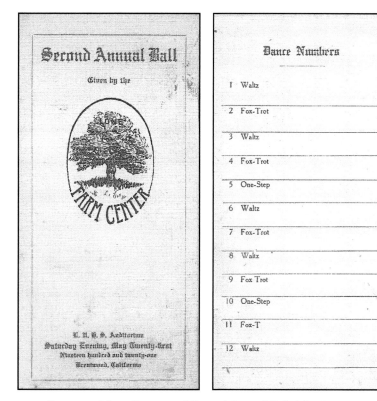

Dance card from Brentwood Second Annual Ball, May 21, 1921
(Charlotte's scrapbook, Author Collection)

CHAPTER 18
The Gem

Philip Lynch
~Brentwood, 1921~

It was Lottie's idea at first, and well, I knew when she brought it up that she'd been thinking about it for a while. We had a couple of good years here on the farm at first, but these past three years sent us into decline when the clouds just stopped raining. One year of no rain, why, that'll cause a farmer some concern; but after the second dry year, you begin to pray even if you're not churchgoing. No water, barely enough for the barley to start in the spring. We were dry farming with no irrigation, and on that second year without rain, 1920, the harvest was too low and we just barely broke even. The third year, 1921, the drought broke us, and broke me of farming forever. The hills were just dry, brown dust with no hope for rain in sight. We had six children by then, with Barbara barely brand new and the rest growing like beanstalks. I still had to make it.

Lottie and I had already gone broke once, six years before, through no fault of our own. That damn scarlet fever robbed me of my youngest son and my livelihood and left us without a dime. There was the quarantine and then Hennessey, my so-called bookkeeper, taking from the till. Now after five years of farming, with that third year of drought, our funds were once again close to zero.

So, when the idea for the theater lease in San Francisco came to me by way of my wife, I began to take to it. We already knew the City, had lived there for almost fifteen years before we moved to the farm. But the hay, grain and coal business I had then wasn't going to feed my family, now that everyone had an automobile. Why, when the money was good here in Brentwood, I went into Sacramento and I bought myself a Ford with isinglass windows you could roll right down, in case there's a change in the weather. Now I could barely put gas in the tank. I'd probably have to sell it soon.

The lease on the theater was one we could afford, $20 a month. Lottie had it figured out right to the penny. "This one's on Ocean Avenue, Phil," she said, pulling out the advertisement she'd cut from last week's *San Francisco Chronicle*. "This one here, it's right in a neighborhood on a busy street. You know how we like to go the movies when we can, even out here in the country in Antioch. But in the City, people might go once or twice a week. See, there's a new movie that comes two times, once on Friday and once on Tuesday. We could make back our investment in no time!"

Well, I did have a passel of kids to put to work. They could all have a job, I thought. I told my wife a few days later, "I've been thinking about your idea—it could work. Walt's old enough at fifteen to run the projection machine in the evenings after school, and Phil Jr. could ride the streetcar to get the movies on Market Street a couple afternoons a week. Camilla, she'll run the player piano. You and I, we'll take tickets and keep the books. Let's look at those figures, again, Mother."

Later that evening, we began to hope once more.

I knew Charlotte missed the City like the dickens. I felt bad for her life here on the farm. It was hard for me to watch her work all day cooking, cleaning, ironing, and then going to play practices at night.

She had always loved the theater. Taught me to love it too. I like a good yarn, and going to the movies makes the story seem so real. I remember going to a nickelodeon movie house in San Francisco and paying five cents a ticket. I guess it was about a year after Walter was born, about 1905, I'd say. Charlotte and I saw *The Great Train Robbery* produced by that fella that started the telegraph, Thomas Edison. The film only lasted about ten minutes or so, but I remember the feeling I had, seeing my first movie; well, it was a funny thing. There were people moving on that screen, but not real people. Like a play, but no talking. You had to put it all together from just the pictures. There was music, dramatic music. I had to wrap my head around and change my notions of what was real. At the end of that

Actor Justus Barnes in *The Great Train Robbery* fires point blank at audience (left).
Film poster, 1903 (right) (Idylease.org)

movie, that bank robber took aim and shot us all, and I'll be darned if everyone—women and men, including me—we all jumped up!

It was a thrill to see those movies. Back then, we had never seen anything like it. After that, Charlotte and I went to the Casino Movie House over in Antioch to see the picture show maybe once every couple of months. We both still enjoyed the live theater, and of course Charlotte loved to act, always had. She'd gotten several good reviews here in the Contra Costa newspapers for her roles in the local playhouse productions. She took such pleasure and fulfillment from it all. Why, this new idea of leasing a silent movie house in the City had put the spark back in her eyes. For me, that was all there was to it. We decided to risk it. I took what little savings I had, got a small loan from her folks, packed up the kids and dog, sold the horses, gave the plows back to my brothers, and moved my family back to the big City by the Bay.

On the way back to San Francisco, I got to thinking. It seemed to me that the 1920s would shape up to be pretty prosperous. Even though our farm didn't pan out, folks in the City were doing well by then. There were lots of new dance halls, and the young ones were putting on different styles, with short skirts for the women, and some fellas not wearing neckties day to day. President Cleveland had passed Prohibition and I have to say, it put the damper on folks' nightlife. I myself stopped drinking all together quite a few years before. I just quit, after my best friend had too much of the drink and died. Why, we were both only thirty-four then, and I said to myself, this is it, it wasn't worth it, and I already had four kids. As I thought about the theater idea, I was leaning toward the likelihood of neighborhood folks like us going out to the movies for entertainment. We'd have to see, it was all so new.

When we got to the City and moved into the rental house on 650 Broderick, a nice walk-up flat near the Panhandle, I began to assess the situation. Most every neighborhood had a small movie house within walking distance, some just storefronts with bed sheets for screens. But the Gem was the real deal, with plush seats, one story, wood framed, and a small area in front for ticket taking.

I began to think it through: Saturday and Sunday matinee tickets would be 5 cents apiece. Evening shows, 10 cents for a first run, 5 cents after that. If we filled up the place, 100 times 10 cents was $10 on a full night. We'd have to run ads in the *San Francisco Chronicle* and the local neighborhood paper. Also, we'd have to pay the once-a-month rent on the movie house to Ed Young. 'Course I wouldn't have to pay the kids, they got free room and board! Jack and Don were still in elementary school and I thought they could watch Barbara pretty well on nights when the rest of us needed to be there, running the show. The movies themselves, why they would be $3 to rent each film, and I had to figure on the piano rolls for player piano. There were different rolls for each type of film: drama, comedy, action, and such. I heard tell of talking pictures coming sometime soon, but until that day, we would do fine with Camilla on the player piano.

We opened the doors to the Gem Theater on July 5, 1921. There was a big grand opening, and I'll be darned if we didn't nearly fill the place. Now that put a smile on my face, I'll tell you. This was going to be swell. When the curtain opened, I was proud of the whole family. The lights got dark, the music started, and Walter flicked the switch on the film reel. The whole audience clapped and cheered, then got real quiet. The feature film was Charlie Chaplin in *The Kid*. Everyone in The Gem went home happy that night, and many subsequent happy times were spent there. I always liked it when we could show a local gal or guy. ZaSu Pitts from Santa Cruz was one of my favorites, although I didn't mention it to my wife. ZaSu

Charlie Chaplin and Jackie Coogan in *The Kid*, 1921 (Wikimedia Commons)

was great, especially in *For the Defense*, a real crime solver. Of course, the comedies were great hits. Laurel and Hardy were favorites, and those two brought tears of laughter to my eyes. Still they all brought in paying customers.

I was concerned about Walt and Camilla because they had the hardest jobs. Also, they had to finish high school in the City, when they'd just been in country schools in Brentwood. I knew they were smart; they always did well in school. As Walter was the oldest at seventeen, he was used to lots of responsibility, like I was. He didn't have nine younger ones coming up behind him like I did, but he had five now, and he was one of the most sensible of all my kids. Never got in trouble in school. Occasionally Miss Violet Trembath sent a note from the Lone Tree School about the younger boys' behavior, but never about Walt. I hoped we could count on him to be on time to get the films on the reel, sync his watch to exactly 7 pm, and flick the projector switch. He had to change film reels from the short to the feature film. Walt was so studious, with his head in a book all the time, that I worried the hours spent in the projection room would hurt his studies. He figured out how to bring a flashlight into the back room while the movie was running so he could study his schoolbooks and check the time. Turns out Walter did fine with all that responsibility, and accepted a scholarship to college two years later.

Camilla was another story. Camilla was in her own world, mostly. I guess it was because she was surrounded by all my boys, two on either side, and she got lonely and a little resentful of all the chores the womenfolk had to do. She complained about ironing the most. When our youngest Barbara arrived, Camilla took to her a bit more than she ever did the boys, but even so, we just never knew what went on in that pretty red head of hers. When Mother and I told Camilla about moving back to the City from Brentwood, she cried and said she'd be so sad to leave her friends at the ranch, and in the same sentence wondered if any movie stars might drop by while we were showing the pictures.

The player piano for the theater had to have an operator, not just someone to put the rolls into the music box. Camilla would stand on the pedals and operate it like a bicycle or a treadle sewing machine. Mother helped her choose the right music for comedy, drama, Westerns and the like. We had both Camilla and Phil Jr. run the player piano. That was a mistake. I am not sure whatever made those two fight like cats and dogs, but they sure had carried on ever since they were born. Even now

The Greatest Piano Value in the World

Advertisement for player pianos, called pianolas, self-playing pianos popular in early 1900s, *The Sun*, Nov 15, 1914 (Library of Congress)

that they were older, they'd bicker until you couldn't hear yourself think! Camilla always said Phil was pumping it too fast, and naturally Phil complained that she was too slow. Yet the player piano was a necessity, to add to the mood and keep the show moving along. So we put them both on it, and somehow we made the best of it. Truth be told, the rhythm on that thing was always a little off, but they got the job done.

About a year after we began at The Gem, I took the streetcar over to the new Castro Theatre, which had just opened, to see what all the fuss was about. Well, it was pretty grand. Kind of rivaled the Opera House, but not up to that standard quite yet. The Castro with its balcony and all could hold 1,400 folks. What a pip! That trip proved to me that movies were the up and coming thing, becoming a regular part of everyone's lives.

(left) Advertisement for Castro Theatre, *San Francisco Chronicle,* June 22, 1922.
(above) Inside the Castro Theatre, 1922 (KQED Arts)

Of course, our Gem Theater was a much smaller affair, but it was grand too, in its own way. Good location, next to my old alma mater, City College, at the crossing of Geneva and Ocean. Even though the Balboa Theater had just opened up eight blocks down the street, most folks walked to the movies. We could host up to 100 in our playhouse. *Not bad, not bad at all,* I said to myself as I added up ticket sales. The frame's solid wood, and it being just one story makes it easy on clean-up after everyone has gone home.

There were many great films in 1922: *Grandma's Boy, Nanook of the North, Sherlock Holmes, Shadow of the Vampire.* Lots of stars, too: Harold Lloyd, Rudolph Valentino, Charlie Chaplin, Hedda Hopper, Dorothy Dalton, Buster Keaton. Oh, Harold Lloyd made me laugh out loud, even better than Charlie Chaplin, I thought, but they were all good, and folks packed the Gem Theater to see them.

Advertisement in *San Francisco Chronicle* for local theaters, The Gem listed in lower right, March 12, 1922

We began to relax, with this movie business steady and the family together. Charlotte was happy to be back in the City. We got comfortable in a way that had eluded us for darn near six years.

We had our worries, of course. Lottie lost her mother that first year in 1922, when Marie Louise was only 63. My wife always had a special bond with her mother, and Lottie seemed lost without her for a time. 'Course my father-in-law Garrett was broken-hearted without his wife. They were a good, devoted couple. Lottie's sister Veda, always so careful and kind-hearted, took good care of them both. Another year we had to pull Jack and Don out of St. Anne's Grammar School. Mother explained it to me; the nuns had told her they were "ruffians from the country" and didn't know how to act right. She told those nuns a thing or two as well, pulled the boys out and put them in the boys-only school in the next parish. They behaved fine from then on. I found my boys easier to handle in the City. I didn't have to prod them to work on the farm, plowing or getting up early to milk. As much as they liked farm life with all their freedom to roam the hills, there were no more surprises like the rodeo stunt they tried to pull off last spring.

We had great times at The Gem. Kids came in for the Saturday matinees and their parents followed in the evenings. We even had a "crying area" for parents of new babies; after seven kids of our own, Lottie and I knew that was a necessity. Folks loved the movies we showed. They hooted and howled against the villains, cried at the love scenes, breathed sighs of relief when the girls were untied from the train tracks, and laughed out loud at the antics of Chaplin and Harold Lloyd.

Meanwhile, Lottie and I counted the ticket sales. Everything was on the up and up. I had no other business partners except my wife and kids. Didn't have to hire help. Walt was so reliable on the reels. We just had to keep Phil and Camilla pumping the piano, and make sure young Jack and Don kept out of mischief and held the fort at home, with little Barbara all in one piece. And I could see it right there in theater listings in the newspaper, and my name right there in the 1922 City Directory, my new profession:

Philip E Lynch, Theater Manager
973 Ocean, San Francisco, California

One afternoon a salesman came by and asked if we might want to sell concessions, food like popcorn and candy bars inside the Gem. He insisted that we could make more than 50% profit. Folks sometimes did bring their own snacks and even dinners into The Gem, but I liked this new idea and the profit margin looked good.

I knew that the latest idea to come along wasn't always the best or most profitable one, but I'd seen big ideas like the automobile come and stay for good. Even when most folks said the Tin Lizzie would never replace our horses, I'd seen their doubt and skepticism fall away fast when they saw how convenient automobiles became to them. All they had to do was fill them up with gasoline; there was no clean-up to the auto and no runaways, unlike your horse that needs constant care, food and attention. So the auto became a part of our daily lives here and everywhere across the nation.

I told Mr. Morrison that we'd consider selling snacks. Talked it over with Lottie, and she loved the idea. That was in December 1922, and we would go ahead with the concessions after the start of the new year.

1923 brought with it the feeling for both of us, really, that we'd used our heads this time. The theater was helping us fill our pockets again, pay the rent, and put food on the table. Charlotte was happy. She began to hold card parties in our flat and was helping out the Ladies' Aid Society. I felt she was in her element again, with farm life far behind her. I still missed the land a bit but was too busy with the family and my new business venture to miss country life that much.

Way back when I was a young man and took over my Uncle Pat's hay, grain and coal business in San Francisco, I knew I'd need some help with the business side of things. Those courses I took at City College gave me the knowledge and confidence that I could enable a business to turn a profit. Now that I was more than twenty years older, I still used my head for business in the day-to-day dealings of The Gem. We had to charge the going rate for tickets, but the popcorn and candy idea would increase our sales to the point where

I thought we might be able to send Phil Jr. and Walter to the University of San Francisco, and Camilla to art school.

I mentioned before that Phil Jr. had the job of exchanging the films from one week to the next. He carried them back and forth on the half-hour ride from The Gem to the Miles Brothers' warehouse on Golden Gate Avenue. I could tell he felt grown up, important, with this task. He'd pick up the finished reels from Walter, who had rewound the film and put the canisters back together. The reels were about twenty inches in diameter, and Phil could carry both the serial and the two main reels on his own. I got to feeling that there was a girl at the front desk of the warehouse that he liked, as he began to leave a little earlier than usual those February mornings. The week before, around Valentine's Day, I overheard him ask Walter what he thought about bringing a girl a heart-shaped box of chocolates. I thought. Phil Jr. was starting a bit young, but he'd always been one to show off for the young ladies. Even on the ranch, he'd dress up with a kerchief and comb his hair on Picnic Day.

I was looking into the candy and concessions idea that week. We could sell those new Baby Ruth and Milky Way bars, and maybe popcorn. Lottie would pop the popcorn at home, hoping my kids wouldn't eat it all before she got to the show. Phil was all set to return the weekend movies and take the streetcar ride out to the Miles Brothers' warehouse on February 6, 1923. That morning, I told him to ask them what other movie houses were selling popcorn and candy, to see what the rest of the theater managers were doing. He set out that Monday after school with Sunday's film, and would come back to The Gem around 5 pm, in plenty of time for us to set up next week's features.

Seventy-One Years Later
~Sacramento Delta, March 1994~

My Uncle Phil told me the story of The Gem in his late eighties. He was driving his red Buick with the white vinyl top along the levees of the Sacramento Delta, giving my family a tour of the old homesteads. Phil was a big, kind man, heavyset, sporting a pork pie hat decorated with fly fishing lures. He wore a tweed sport coat, white shirt and no tie. He talked to the four of us, my mother Barbara, my daughters Katie and Emily, and me, in an easy fashion. He had been a travelling salesman and always had a story to tell his clients.

Now as we rolled along, he told us about that day: February 6, 1923.

"'Course, my job for the Gem was to go on the streetcar and carry the film safely back and forth from Ocean Street to Golden Gate Avenue. Those canisters were some big reels! Walt had them all rewound by the time I'd pick them up at The Gem the night before. The nuns gave me special permission to leave the film reels in the cloakroom, so I could get them after school for the streetcar ride. Of course we left the serials in the canisters at the theater, as they were smaller than the main reels, and the studio sent us enough for the full week.

"As I recall, a couple of secretaries had caught my eye back in those days, so I was happy to take the half-hour ride to get to the film exchange just to talk with them, you know. My dad wanted me to ask the fellas there about the concessions idea that day too. I had a little chat with the gals and the head bosses, who told me that other theaters were starting to sell food inside their movie houses too, a swell idea. I picked up the new films and was on my way down Market Street, then transferred to Ocean for the short trip on the M Line. As the streetcar approached The Gem, I heard the conductor give a low whistle, then he said, 'Whoa, Phil, look! Look there ahead, your theater, it's gone!'"

"What the hell?' I shouted. Sure enough, The Gem was gone! Smoke was smoldering around the edges of the wooden building. Our family's theater had burned to the ground!

"I hurried on home to see that my mother and father had already heard. Dad was on the telephone to Mr. Ed Young to see if either of them had insurance for this type of disaster. No dice. My dad was out of work that very day. We all tried to pitch in after that as much as we could…" and Phil's voice trailed off into the morning Delta air.

(left) Article from *San Francisco Chronicle*, Feb 6, 1923;
(right) article from Lottie's scrapbook about the Gem fire, (Author Collection)

Barbara Mahoney

~Santa Cruz, California~

I talked to my mother one afternoon in 2014, when she was ninety-four years old, about the Gem fire and their lives afterwards. Her memory was crystal clear.

"When the theater burned down," she said, "my mother pawned her wedding ring just so they could stay afloat. Your sister Sue wears my mother's new ring, the one we all gave them years later, on their fiftieth wedding anniversary. But they sure had some tough times then, some tough times…"

She shook her head. "My dad always had jobs after the theater burned. He worked putting up billboards. He'd help build houses, run delivery trucks, anything he could find. For several years in the 1930s, during the early part of the Depression, he worked as a private Special Policeman in the City, along the Panhandle of Golden Gate Park. He carried a gun for that job. Every night when he came home, he put the gun in his top drawer. He told us never, ever, ever to touch it, and by God we didn't!

"As I look back now, I believe Mother suffered from depression and shock. I think she had too many disappointments, really, so she turned me over to him. My dad practically raised me. I am so much like him because we spent so much time together."

She went on, "I remember when Dad was a Special Policeman. He'd take me on his rounds to collect from the homeowners and businessmen who contracted with him to guard their places. I was about eight and nine. The businessmen would give me candy and Dad would take me to Blum's afterwards for ice cream. One Valentine's Day I got a real cut valentine from one of them; I'd never seen such fancy cards! On Dad's days off he took me to the Fleishhacker Zoo to see the bears. He and I had great times together. Yet, we were dirt poor. I grew up in many houses in the City, as Mother liked to move around a lot. You didn't question it, you moved, and that was it.

"Once we had a bigger house in the hills at Tenth and Kirkham. We lived with all the family, my Aunt Veda, Grandpa Smith and Veda's son Glen, all eleven of us together. But even in that big house, I never had a room of my own. Because I was the youngest, I always slept in a little closet or on a cot in my parents' room. My sister Camilla always had her own room, and my brothers must have shared rooms. Looking back on our lives, it wasn't easy. My mother sewed all my clothes, as we never had money for store-bought clothes. When we had dress-up day once a month at our Catholic school, I didn't have new clothes like the rest of the girls.

"It really hit me," she continued, "when I was in seventh grade. I'd visit the houses of my school-mates in the Upper Haight. These girls' families had pianos in their living rooms and maids to help their parents with chores, and they always had new clothes. We had none of that. Dad took the boys hunting in Stern Grove for rabbits and such, and they went to Lake Merced to fish and shoot ducks for our dinner. Many times, there were pheasants and mallards in the bathtub waiting to be plucked.

"My brothers, Jack and Don, had to quit high school just to help support the family. Later on, Jack went to work on Market Street selling shoes and sporting goods. Don did get his certificate to sell insurance a few years after high school, and was in the insurance business the rest of his life. My brother Phil took courses at Golden Gate College and the University of San Francisco for law, but was unable to finish. Walt got through college in 1928 and went on to become a lawyer. My brothers and sister were smart, capable people.

"I have to say, in the end of their lives, my mom and dad were never bitter about their lot. They persevered, and enjoyed their family all the way through."

CHAPTER 19
Capitola and San Francisco

All my life I heard the story of The Gem and the sad fate that my grandparents' theater burned to the ground. After all these hard times, one would think that the fire would have been the straw that broke the camel's back. But no matter how many times my grandparents were down—through a deadly train wreck, the 1906 earthquake, their baby's death, the farm drought, and now The Gem's quick and early demise—they kept on with life.

During their later years in Capitola and San Francisco, Lottie and Philip were quite busy with their growing family. They kept their spirits up by living their lives in the ways that had seen them through so many challenging times before—hard work and the resolve to keep going as a family and as couple. Each of them found ways to recharge themselves.

Lottie loved to cook for her family. She used her skills in the kitchen to provide hot popovers for my mother and her friends after school and baked cookies, pies and cakes several times a week. Her sweet tooth remained with her all of her life.

My grandmother also took time to relax and rejuvenate in the security of her childhood home in Isleton on the banks of the Sacramento River. My mother Barbara fondly recalls travelling on the *Delta Queen* and *Delta King* steamboats with her mother Lottie in the 1920s and '30s, leaving the San Francisco Ferry Building at five in the evening and arriving at the Smith's private dock

Postcard, the River Lines, daily from San Francisco to Sacramento
(Courtesy of the California History Room, California State Library, Sacramento, CA)

early the next morning. In those days, a round trip fare cost $3. Barbara in her later years did not know how her mother saved enough for the both of them to make those trips. They brought their dinner packed from home and did not eat in the fancy dining room aboard ship.

Barbara also fondly recalls that her Aunt Veda was an excellent seamstress and made Barbara seven dresses, one for each day of the week, to wear to her first days of kindergarten. Veda, who lived in the Delta then, most likely purchased the pins, needles and bolts of cloth from K. Nakano's Dry Goods Store in Isleton's Japantown. The Delta had a large Japanese population and many people of Japanese descent worked hard in the fields and town.

Lottie always took great pleasure in her elocutionary skills. Of course, since she had memorized many titles from her school years and early twenties, she was able to recite these memorized poems with accuracy and drama. One of her favorites was the classic American poem "Casey at the Bat," which she recited as a duet with her son, Walt.

On his days off, Philip often took his growing sons to the Delta to hunt ducks and wildfowl, as he had when he was a boy in the latter part of the 1880s and 1890s. At that time the skies over the Delta's inland waterways were still filled with so many birds that they would blacken the skies during their migrations. The waterfowl were still present in high numbers in the 1920s and '30s, although beginning to decline. Philip and his sons also hunted rabbits and quail on the outskirts of San Francisco, at nearby Lake Merced and the Crystal Springs Reservoir.

The Great Depression began in October of 1929, just six years after the family's theater business went up in flames, and lasted until 1940. Those long years spent under the shadow of the Depression and the extreme economic hardships it brought to the whole country were unceasingly hard on the family. Lottie, Camilla and Barbara made their own coats and dresses. Barbara's first store-bought coat came to her on the occasion of her high school graduation in 1938, when her mother had saved up enough money to take her to one of the department stores on Market Street for a new blue coat.

Given the country was still in the throes of the Depression, the only Lynch child to finish college was the oldest, Walter, who received a full scholarship to the University of San Francisco and later earned his law degree from there as well. Phil Jr. also earned a scholarship to attend law school but was unable to finish his degree. He kept his law books most all of his life.

There were happy times in the midst of these years. Jack and Phil bought an RCA Victrola record player and the teenagers would dance the jitterbug to the tunes of Duke Ellington, Count Basie and the Big Band sounds in the basements of their homes. Barbara remembers that her brothers and sister had parties when their folks were away visiting relatives in the Delta. Her siblings smuggled alcohol into the house during the Prohibition years of the early 1930s, serving gin-filled watermelons to their guests. Camilla was able to get hand-me-down flapper clothes from her cousins, the Hodapps, across the Bay in Piedmont. Barbara remembers being the younger kid upstairs when her sister and brothers brewed alcohol in the bathtub, then tried their best to cover up the evidence before their parents arrived back home.

Barbara and some of her high school friends walked across the brand-new Golden Gate Bridge with thousands of others on its opening

Lottie and Philip Lynch, San Francisco, each with a brace of ducks from Victoria Island, Sacramento Delta, circa 1930s
(Author Collection)

day of May 27, 1937. The long, elegant suspension bridge would become an iconic part of the City, and was later declared a Wonder of the Modern World by the American Society of Civil Engineers. Barbara remembers that San Francisco was different back then when she was growing up. It felt safe to her, and she and her friends never hesitated to walk in Golden Gate Park, even at night.

Camilla and Barbara were both, like their mother, talented artists. Camilla went to art school after high school, which she attended at night for just one year until she had an accident, catching her hand in the wringer of a washing machine. This damaged her drawing hand, and she was unable to paint after that. In 1937, Camilla and her dad went to work at the new San Francisco Mint, where they helped in the production of coins for general circulation.

Golden Gate Bridge, opening day, May 1937
(Author Collection)

Both of them remembered that workers were searched coming and going, wore special clothing at work, and had to shower before leaving. Those showers had special drains to catch any metal residue a worker might be carrying, either deliberately or unwittingly.

Barbara was an excellent student, and the nuns at St. Agnes Elementary School saw that she could be college-bound. They encouraged her to go to Presentation High School, one of the private Catholic schools in San Francisco. However, Barbara would have had to work as a secretary in the convent in exchange for her tuition, and she, in her proud way, said no thanks. She went on to graduate from the free public Polytechnic High School. Barbara went to work for Spiro's Sporting Goods Store on Market Street in the City for a couple of years, then was employed by the United States government as a secretary in the beginning of World War II. She quit that job when she married my father, Pat Mahoney, a PGA golf professional, in May of 1942.

Lottie's mother Marie Louise had died at 63 in 1922, but Lottie's father, Garrett Smith, lived well into his nineties. Garrett was able to produce enough pears and asparagus to keep his ranch going through the 1920s. However, later in the Depression years, he was unable to make ends meet on the ranch. He leased his land in 1936 to Bing Chong, whose family had worked on Delta farms since the 1920s. Bing's brother, Look Chong, purchased the Garrett Smith ranch in 1941. Garrett and his daughter Veda moved to Redwood City, on the San Francisco Peninsula.

During World War II, Charlotte and Phil's youngest son Jack signed up for the Merchant Marines, was shipped to Australia, and there met his future wife, Joan. It was a tremendous relief to Charlotte and Philip when Jack returned safely. Their two sons-in-law, Camilla's husband Jack and Barbara's husband Pat, were both

Look Chong, top right, purchased Garrett Smith's ranch in 1936 (By permission, private collection, Darryl and Ronald Chong)

drafted, but returned home safely to their wives and families in 1944. None of the other Lynch sons were drafted.

Charlotte and Philip's lives took on a new dimension when they became grandparents. Their family remained close. In the late 1940s and early 1950s, there were family reunions on holidays, bringing the six Lynch siblings and their spouses together. Lottie and Philip had fourteen grandchildren: Patsy, Nancy, Margaret, Sharon, Philip, Donna, Lorene, Lois, Donny, Sherry, Kathy, Pat, Sue and Jean. All the grandkids had many happy times on weekends and holidays visiting their grandparents' homes, where they played Tiddlywinks and helped their grandmother cook. Philip rode the streetcar with his grandchildren to visit Golden Gate Park and Stern Grove, and took them to see the sights downtown in the City. Their eldest granddaughter Patsy recalls riding up and down the escalator in the Emporium Department store over and over again while her patient grandparents waited on either end for her to return. Nancy remembers the times she spent at their homes in the summers and says with true conviction that Grandpa always "favored the youngest, whoever that might be at the time."

Charlotte Lynch, Sunset District, San Francisco, circa 1940s (Author Collection)

Their granddaughter Sharon recalls spending time with both grandparents in the City and has warm recollections of her time with them. Philip Jr., the fourth Philip in the family line, remembers spending time with his grandpa playing par three golf in Golden Gate Park. Phil Jr. remembers going duck hunting with his father, Philip, and his uncles Walter, Jack and Don in the Sacramento Delta, getting up early with them and bearing witness to their stories of life on the Brentwood farm.

Grandchildren Donna, Lorene and Lois, who spent their childhoods across the Golden Gate Bridge in Marin County, all recall great times with their Grandpa and their grandmother, who they called Nana. Donna held tea parties in honor of Lottie, who had passed the art of the tea party on to her redheaded granddaughter. Lorene and Lois spent happy hours playing in the dollhouse their grandpa built for them with his own two hands.

Philip Lynch carving Thanksgiving turkey in Capitola with daughter Barbara, circa 1946 (Author Collection)

In the late 1940s, my parents Barbara and Pat moved to Santa Cruz when my father was hired as head golf pro at the Pasatiempo Golf Course. My grandparents Lottie and Philip also moved to help with our growing family. My mother helped them rent a small farm in Capitola on Rosedale Avenue, where Philip cared for horses and chickens and grew vegetables in the small coastal garden. He helped care for his four-year-old grandson Pat and three-year-old granddaughter Sue. Both clearly remember their grandpa hanging several rattlesnakes on the hillside, having killed them with a shovel to keep the family safe. Sue recalls that her grandparents were both fun-loving and easy to be with.

My brother Pat has vivid memories of his grandpa letting him ride the Capitola farm horse up the hill on Rosedale Avenue. Four-year-old Pat was in full cowboy regalia, sure

Pat Mahoney, 1946, on Grandpa Philip Lynch's horse in Capitola (Author Collection)

that he was the spitting image of Hopalong Cassidy, when the horse began to gallop. Grandpa ran beside him, shouting, "Grab the reins, Pat! Grab the reins!" Pat didn't know what he meant, so he just jumped off the horse, landing on his own two feet, much to his grandpa's relief.

My family returned to San Francisco after two years, when my father was hired as head golf pro at Lake Merced Golf Club. Philip and Lottie followed their youngest daughter back to the City, living out their lives in San Francisco. They rented houses in the Sunset District and visited their children's families frequently. Charlotte served tea with her granddaughters. All of their grandchildren have fond memories of our grandparents' unconditional love and recall happy times spent in the care of their Nana and Grandpa.

In her later years, Lottie took up oil painting once again, and to this day many of her later works reside in the homes of her grandchildren and great-grandchildren. She was always a voracious reader and filled many days reading authors of the day, such as *Cannery Row* by John Steinbeck and *Suds In Your Eye* by Mary Lasswell. Her heart's delight continued to be the closeness she felt in the presence of her daughters and sons. She still loved card games and challenged her mind with games of solitaire.

On February 21, 1953, Charlotte and Philip Lynch celebrated their golden fiftieth wedding anniversary at the Fairmont Hotel in San Francisco. Philip was seventy-six and his bride Lottie just sixty-eight years old. Their whole family was there: six adult children and their spouses, their grandchildren, and many old friends. They were joined by eighty guests. My three-year old cousin Lois and I (at 2 ½) proudly walked up an aisle to greet our seated grandparents. I presented my grandmother with a brand-new wedding ring, which my grandpa had bought for her from his savings. My sister Sue wears that ring to this day. The fiftieth anniversary day is one all present remembered with great fondness. The couple's eldest son, Walter, read aloud an original poem about their lives and adventures. It was time to reflect on the couple's fortitude, history, and resolve.

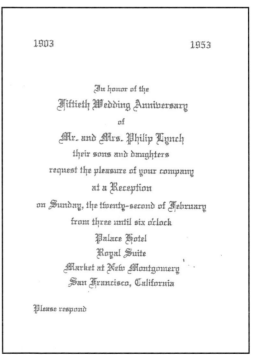

1903   1953

In honor of the
Fiftieth Wedding Anniversary
of
Mr. and Mrs. Philip Lynch
their sons and daughters
request the pleasure of your company
at a Reception
on Sunday, the twenty-second of February
from three until six o'clock
Palace Hotel
Royal Suite
Market at New Montgomery
San Francisco, California

Please respond

Charlotte & Philip's 50th wedding anniversary invitation (Author Collection)

Philip and Charlotte are beaming in the black-and-white photograph that commemorates this occasion, surrounded by all of their family. The day before, they had been featured in a *San Francisco Chronicle* article about their golden anniversary. Charlotte saved this article in her scrapbook, as she had faithfully done all her life. When asked the secret to their remarkable fifty-year partnership, she and Phillip told the reporter that "patience and consideration" were the foundation of their happy marriage

The next year, on June 13, 1954, at the age of sixty-nine, Charlotte passed away suddenly from a heart attack while playing an afternoon game of cards with her son, Phil Jr., and his wife Alyce. My mother Barbara had always been close with her father, and Philip moved in with our family on 42nd Avenue in San Francisco. There my parents built him a bedroom and bathroom in private quarters downstairs. In the evening he retired early to listen to his favorite radio show, *One Man's Family*, the story of a San Francisco family, the most popular and longest running national serial of the time.

Of course, Philip missed Lottie deeply. He kept busy visiting Golden Gate Park with his grandchildren and sometimes spent nights

Charlotte and Philip's 50th anniversary, surrounded by 11 of 14 grandchildren, 1953. L to R: Sharon, Pat, Margie, Jean, Nancy, Lois, Patsy, Sue, Philip, Donna, Lorene. Three more grandchildren, Donny, Kathy and Sherry, were born after this event (Author Collection)

MR. AND MRS. PHILIP LYNCH
Then came autos and gas.

★ ★ ★

Couple Marking Golden Wedding

The Philip Lynches Recall Early Days

Patience and consideration are the foundation of 50 years of happy marriage, Philip and Charlotte Lynch, of 817 36th-av, declared today on the eve of their golden wedding anniversary.

Tomorrow afternoon at the Palace Hotel with their four sons, two daughters, 11 grandchildren and some 80 guests they will recount the highlights of their years together.

Spry, 70-year-old Philip Lynch recalls his youth spent in hot, sun-baked grain fields around Brentwood, Contra Costa County. Equally vivid are his recollections of hunting rabbits and quail, in what is now St. Francis Wood, near the turn of the century.

In Feed Business

Lynch was in the coal and feed business for 20 years here, spent five years ranching and returned to work in the new Mint before he retired.

"The introduction of gas killed our coal business and the development of the automobile spelled the end of our feed trade," he said.

Recalls Rail Wreck

Mrs. Lynch remembered that three months after they were married they were in a railroad wreck near Point Reyes and the prospects of ever celebrating a 50th anniversary were dim, indeed.

The younger members of the Lynch clan who will help their folks celebrate tomorrow include E. Walter Lynch, an attorney of Pittsburg; Philip G. Lynch, in the sports goods business here; Mrs. John Loughman; Donald Lynch, insurance broker; Jack Lynch, a sports goods salesman and distributor, and Mrs. Barbara Mahoney, wife of Pat Mahoney, golf pro.

San Francisco Chronicle article, Philip and Charlotte's 50th anniversary, February 21, 1953 (Charlotte's scrapbook, Author Collection) in Marin County with his son Don's family, where he designed and built a playhouse for his granddaughters. Every morning my grandfather rose early to make hot biscuits for our family. I remember these mornings with great fondness, reading the funny papers from the *San Francisco Chronicle* while sitting on Grandpa's lap.

Philip planned to attend my fifth birthday party in Mill Valley on June 28, 1955, but said he didn't feel well and stayed home. He passed away from a heart attack the very next day, at seventy-eight years old, while playing golf at Harding Park Golf Course in the City. He and Charlotte are buried next to one another at the Holy Cross Cemetery in Colma, just south of San Francisco.

My mother Barbara reminisced, "My father loved all of you very much. I remember that he built playhouses and dollhouses for his grandkids."

"I remember that playhouse he built for Lois," I replied. "I wanted one too, but he didn't get to build me one."

"Yes," she said with her sharp memory, "but he was always up early when he lived with us in his last year, making biscuits, playing with you."

"He was my first friend," I told her with the certainty that only a four-year-old has. "We both got up early together." She nodded, probably glad back then that someone got up at 6:30 am with me.

"I can still see him," I told her. "He had his white hair combed just right, spectacles on, wearing a nice white shirt covered over by his soft brown sweater with leather buttons. He got up first, I heard him, and I tiptoed out of my room down the hall and left Sue still sleeping. We read the funnies in the papers and ate warm biscuits with butter and jam. Then we went out to play in the sandbox."

"Oh, you two were quite a pair, making mud pies and tracking sand into the house!"

"Yes, Grandpa was my first friend," I said again, "and as his youngest grandchild, I guess I was his last friend. I missed him so. I will always remember walking down the stairs to his room that day he died, to see if he could play. He wasn't there, but a pack of Lifesavers was tucked into the stairwell all wrapped up, just for me."

Philip Lynch with granddaughter, author Jean Mahoney, 1953 (Author Collection)

My mother nodded, "My dad died right there on Harding Park Golf Course. I think he scared my brother Jack half to death. He hit a great tee shot, had a heart attack, and died five minutes later."

"I missed him," I said again.

"I missed him too," she replied.

My mother continued to recall her parents' times over their long lives, particularly their biggest loss. "When Russell caught scarlet fever and died," she said, "the whole family was quarantined in the Burlingame house for six weeks. It was quite a predicament. Just two months before, they had six healthy children. Now they had only five. Well, I think that was the hardest time for both of them. But my dad liked to work, and he did have a good idea of how to get his family out of all those troubles."

My grandparents got out of all their troubles with the strength they took from each other. My grandmother, the vivacious Lottie Smith Lynch, had taken my grandfather Philip's heart from that first day they met at Amy's boarding house in downtown San Francisco. Lottie's love of life and pure excitement about the future brought a gust of fresh air to his heart. He grabbed onto this renewal, and held on to her. He enjoyed his wife's creative endeavors, her love of painting, her recitations, her performances on stage, through all their long half-century together. And she relied on him for his calm and steady manner. The way Philip approached each of their troubles was a study in patience, perseverance and consideration. All of his children could see these quaities, and relied upon them as they faced life's ups and downs.

Every life has a story. I have loved getting to know my grandmother Lottie and my grandfather Philip in their younger days. The experiences my grandparents shared, from the ordinary to the extraordinary, reflect their times, and their grit and determination to survive and thrive. Their stories helped me find and bring to life Lottie's parents, Marie Louise and Garrett Smith, and her long, strong line from Ireland, Margaret Anson, Ellen McCrow and Patrick Anson. To learn of these pioneer immigrant's lives and to write their stories educated and inspired me.

Charlotte's and Philip's lives, and as well as their ancestors' lives, are a tribute to the courage and strength that humans possess during good times and hard times. In reading these tales, you have witnessed their willingness to answer the extraordinary challenges presented to them.

Or, as Charlotte's youngest daughter Barbara would say of her parents and of all of her ancestors, "They got the job done."

Charlotte and Philip Lynch surrounded by children, spouses and grandchildren, on their
50th wedding anniversary, February 22, 1953 at Palace Hotel, San Francisco.

TOP, L-R: Nancy Lynch, Joan Lynch, Jack Lynch, Pat Mahoney, Barbara Mahoney, Walter Lynch, Elva
Lynch, Don Lynch, Lefa Lynch, Alyce Lynch, Phil Lynch, Camilla Loughman, Jack Loughman, Patsy Lynch.

CENTER: Charlotte Lynch, Philip Lynch.

BOTTOM: Pat Mahoney, Margaret Lynch, Jean Mahoney, Philip Lynch, Sharon Lynch,
Lois Lynch, Sue Mahoney, Lorene Lynch, Donna Lynch

Epilogue
The Paintings of Charlotte Marie Smith Lynch

My grandmother learned to paint at St. Gertrude's Academy in Rio Vista. Her children and grandchildren had the privilege of having her paintings in their homes as a special part of their daily lives. Many of us still have her paintings on our walls to enjoy and admire our heritage.

Following are just a few of my grandmother's paintings. Some were completed when she was just sixteen years old. The last one included here is from her later years, when she was painting often in her fifties and sixties. My mother says that some of her mother's earliest paintings

CORNER OF PAINTING STUDIO.

Painting studio at St. Gertrude's Academy, where Charlotte learned to paint, circa 1900. One of Charlotte's floral paintings is second from right (Rio Vista Museum)

151

were lost, when they burned in household fires that were, sadly, common to homes in the Delta when my grandmother was young.

A few of these paintings are registered in the Smithsonian Archives of Early American Painters. All paintings below are oil on canvas.

Please enjoy these as we have for so many years.

"Lady in Charcoal" 1902, Charlotte Marie Smith (Family Collection)

"Lillies" 1902, Charlotte Marie Smith (Family Collection)

"The Fortune Teller" 1902, Charlotte Marie Smith (Author Collection)

This oil painting was completed in early 1950s, when
Charlotte was in her late sixties (Family Collection)

Note to Reader

This book focuses on the lives of my Irish immigrant family, their children, grandchildren and great-grandchildren. Yet before Europeans arrived, California was densely populated with diverse tribal peoples speaking over 100 languages. These people lived on the land we call California for many thousands of years.

For hundreds of generations, they were here. They lived in balance and harmony with nature and thrived in the abundance that was offered to them. They witnessed the sun rising over the Bay, saw the same waves crash on the Pacific, drank from the big rivers flowing snowmelt down from the Sierra Nevada Mountains, and breathed in the same fog that caresses our gigantic redwoods. They raised their children, grieved their dead, rejoiced in love and family, preserved and passed down their spiritual traditions, made beautiful art, and crafted daily implements from the lush world around them.

Sadly, the waves of Europeans who arrived in North America, including my ancestors, were part of a process that decimated these local peoples. By the mid-19th century, the Tribes of the Indian Nation had tragically declined in population from the effects of diseases and wars that arose from clashes with the newly arrived Europeans for territory and land. California tribes were markedly displaced from their homelands by the Spanish missionaries who came there to convert the native peoples to Catholicism in the mid 18th century. Tribes were forced to move off of their lands and were conscripted into forced labor.

When my great-great-grandparents came to settle in the San Francisco Bay Area in the 1860's, the city had grown so exponentially after the Gold Rush that there was little evidence that Indian tribes had lived there so long. Still, when I was a young girl in the 1960s, I saw massive Indian shell mounds, on the yet-to-be-developed East Bay waterfront in Emeryville. These mounds were up to 60 feet high and 350 feet in diameter. Over 500 shell mounds were once all around the Bay Area. They contained evidence of the original peoples' culture, such as shells, animal and human remains, ceremonial objects and other artifacts. Now those mounds are mostly gone, having been replaced by shopping centers, houses and office buildings, which stand on streets called Shell-mound Street and Ohlone Way. These shell mounds were close to village sites.

The original peoples of this land must be honored and recognized. The San Francisco Bay Area included the Ohlone, the Coast Miwok and Bay Miwok peoples. Both the Ohlone and Miwok peoples were organized into many small independent tribes located all throughout the entire region, in every place my ancestors lived. The descendants of these original peoples are alive today, and it is my hope and wish that you will learn their stories to hear the timbre of their voices and the outlook of their cultures as well. All who live on the land of the Americas now and in the past can connect to story and land as our common bond.

Acknowledgments

Writing a book is harder than I thought, and more fulfilling than I ever imagined. No part of this book would have been possible without the help of two main people in my life. The first is my mother Barbara Mahoney, who told me these stories over many years. Her encouragement, belief in my talents and practical love of her own family shines through every word. Three weeks before she died I had the great satisfaction of handing her the very last chapter of this book. I sat beside her and watched her read until she turned the last page and closed the cover. It was then I heard her quietly exclaim, "Yes, that's it. You've got it. Very nice." This was high praise from her 97-year-old perspective. Thanks, Ma.

My wife Carolyn Brigit Flynn has been equally supportive. She steadfastly held the vision for the possibilities of this book. It is because of her tenacity, love and encouragement that these stories have come to be written down. It was in Carolyn's writing group twenty years ago that I first wrote the story about my grandmother Lottie coming to San Francisco as a young woman. Throughout the years Carolyn believed that I could do this, and has offered her sharp mind and heart to the writing, editing and production of these pages. Carolyn is one of the reasons that my ancestors' voices speak here. Thanks, Love.

My brother Pat Mahoney and sister Sue Bowers have read parts of this book, and were by my side with advice from their good brains and points of view that only growing up in the same family can give. Thanks to them and to all my cousins, most especially to my cousin Nancy Basque. Without Nancy's excellent genealogical research, this book would not have been written. Nancy was always there with insight as to the facts uncovered during her years-long pursuit of our ancestor's travels and stories.

No book is complete without editors. Melody Culver has been *Brave Hearts* copy-editor over these years. Her keen eye for detail and skill in how things should be done has helped immeasurably. Thanks, Mel.

My daughters Katie Moorehead and Emily Lancaster are the lights in my life that keep shining with encouragement and love. Thanks to both of you.

There are several people who read this book prior to publication. Kate Aver Avraham, Mary Thomas, Melody Culver, and many writers in Carolyn Brigit Flynn's writing groups over the past years have given me feedback, keen insight and ongoing support. Thanks to all.

There are authors who I met along the way who have written about their families and people in historical fiction. I am grateful to Lisa See, who wrote the stories of her Chinese ancestors in her book *On Gold Mountain.* Early on she encouraged me to write and set out the tales of my people. Another author is Shelton Johnson, an African American Park Ranger in Yosemite National Park. Shelton's book *Gloryland* details the life of one of the Buffalo Soldiers in the Civil War. When I met him in Yosemite, he was positive and certain that I should write about my Irish immigrant family.

Fran Shimozaki has been an excellent support and given me information about her Japanese American family in Isleton. We met in the Sacramento Delta, at a time when we were both in search of our ancestors' stories.

Then there are the ones who came before. They always are here with me saying, "Go ahead, just write. Look us up when you can, then just know, know we are proud to be here with you now. We are glad to let everyone know that we lived like you all. Now you know our tales."

I am grateful that they lived such courageous lives with their brave hearts lighting the way.

Sources and References

The following are explanations for the reader to clarify the sources and references I used as information for each chapter. Some of the sources were published history, family documents and internet sites, many were passed down through oral history, and other sources come from the faith that my ancestors have in me.

Chapter 1: For the Hope of It All

The stories of Margaret Fahey Anson and Ellen McCrow and their families are based on the meticulous research done by my cousin Nancy Basque. From the historical records that she uncovered, I knew the family names, the dates of many of their arrivals in America, towns they lived in and when they lived there. I also gathered information on the Irish famine and Irish conditions in those years from the knowledge that my spouse, Carolyn Brigit Flynn, has amassed over her years of study and research on her own Irish ancestors. The rest was gleaned from historical records of those times in local newspapers and records. The quote about Muscatine in 1849 is from a journal article: "Major Williams' Journal of a Trip to Iowa in 1849," *Annals of Iowa,* Vol. XII (1920), p. 249.

Chapter 2: Patrick, Anna and the Civil War

Again, Nancy Basque's research on Margaret, Patrick and Anna Anson is the basis for this chapter. Nancy obtained from the Muscatine Library the original ledger Patrick Anson wrote in his own hand of all the transactions he made while he was guardian for the three McCrow sisters.

This ledger gave us both great satisfaction because we could hold the actual penned words of our great-great-grandfather in our own hands. In addition, the regiments of the Civil War kept precise and excellent records of battles they fought and locations of those regiments. These documentations were found on the internet.

Chapter 3: City by the Bay

My mother, Barbara Mahoney, told me that her great-grandfather Patrick Anson came from Cashel, County Tipperary, Ireland. He immigrated to the United States and moved to Iowa where he married his wife, Anna. After his service in the Civil War, the Ansons moved to San Francisco. My mother had also heard that Patrick Anson was called "Captain Anson" and that her mother, Charlotte Lynch, had seen a picture of him in his Civil War uniform.

My mother and I conjectured that her great-grandparents Patrick and Anna had sailed "round the Horn" from Iowa, leaving Muscatine and traveling down the Mississippi River to the Gulf of Mexico, then all the way around the Cape of Good Hope in South America, and up the Pacific Ocean into the Golden Gate to the City of San Francisco. My mother said she never heard about them crossing by covered wagon nor going through the Isthmus of Panama, both of which were most likely the more dangerous routes of the three choices they had. The cross-country railroad across the United States was not completed until 1868, four years after they made their long journey to the West.

My cousin Nancy Basque's summary of our family history, "The Immigrants," documents that Patrick Anson's brother Richard moved to San Francisco with his wife in 1862. It also documents that Patrick Anson was an officer in the Civil War in Iowa and served for nine months. I concluded that Richard would have written to his brother, urging him to come out West to San Francisco for a better life. I wrote the letter you have read based on this conjecture.

I imagined that Anna Anson gladly would have attended the many offerings of lectures, theater and shows in San Francisco in the late 1860s, such as Mark Twain's public lecture. There were no movie theaters at the time, so folks would go out on the town to be entertained by live performances. Before Mark Twain took his author's name, he had lived and worked on the banks of the Mississippi River near Muscatine where Anna and Patrick lived, working as a riverboat captain under his birth name Samuel Clemens. He lived in Muscatine for one summer in 1855, where his brother Orion published the local newspaper just a few blocks from the Anson's painting store in that town. From researching those times, I came to realize that Anna and Patrick may have known of Mark Twain in the small town of Muscatine, and that for a few years he also lived in San Francisco when they were there, writing as a columnist for several San Francisco journals and newspapers.

Mark Twain did indeed give a lecture on the Sandwich Islands in San Francisco in October of 1866. It was his first-ever public speaking event.

Chapter 4: Coming of Age in San Francisco

Marie Louise's story is based on oral history, as well as historical research on San Francisco in those times. My mother told me many times over that her grandmother Marie Louise was married to a man named Benjamin Garrett and got a divorce from him when her mother, Charlotte, referred to as Lottie, was a baby. Marie Louise went on to marry her second husband, Garrett Smith, several years later. My mother told me that Charlotte grew up in the Sacramento Delta on Garrett Smith's asparagus and pear ranch. My mother also told me that her grandmother, Marie Louise, was a dressmaker and sewed her daughter Charlotte's wedding dress. We conjectured together that Marie Louise may have met Garrett Smith during a dressmaking commission with the Smith family in Isleton.

Chapter 5: Up the Sacramento River

My mother told me that her mother Charlotte was sent away to St. Gertrude's Academy for Girls boarding school partly because her mother, Marie Louise, did not like her playing with the Chinese children whose parents worked on their pear and asparagus ranch. In those days the societal customs were such that whites did not mix with Chinese. A federal law called the "Chinese Exclusion Act" was adopted in 1882. This Act made it illegal for Chinese laborers to come to the United States, which reflected and enforced this segregation. This placed an extraordinary hardship on all the Chinese workers already in California, who made up a large number of the laborers building the railroads and working on farms in the Sacramento Delta and throughout the West. This decade was the time when Charlotte was a young girl and would have naturally played with children her age. In my experience, my grandmother never showed prejudice towards other groups throughout her life.

When I first started to investigate our family's history in the East Bay and Sacramento Delta, I asked my Uncle Phil, "How did we get the land?" referring to Garrett Smith's acreage along the Sacramento River in Isleton and my great-grandfather Philip Lynch's 1,000 acres in the hills of Brentwood. Uncle Phil's reply was quick and unequivocal. "Ah, hell, honey,'" he said, "we stole it! We stole it from the Indians and the Mexicans." I could tell that Uncle Phil had thought this over, and indeed he was right. The Delta land of several hundred acres was deeded to Garrett Smith by the United States government in 1865. They had taken control of this land from the original Mexican land grant called "Rancho Los Medanos." Before the land grant was in Mexican hands, this land had been occupied for thousands of years by the Native American Indian tribes of the Patwin and Coastal Miwok. The history of the people who lived and worked on these lands had been in flux since the years of European and Asian exploration beginning in the 1700s. I concluded that since our ancestors were white European males, they assumed their status and were able to buy land based on this historical privilege.

Chapter 6: The Delta

The only fact I knew from family history was that Garrett Smith rowed solo to pick up his daughter Lottie for Christmas vacation. My Uncle Phil told me this story and emphasized that Garrett's pocket watch had gotten soaked, and never ran again since that day.

I was also able to get the name of the Mother Superior of St Gertrude's from the book *Images of America Rio Vista*. It was interesting to find out that the Mother Superior's name was Sister Camillus, as my grandmother named her first daughter Camilla.

When I was a young girl, I had memories of Garrett Smith spending the Christmas holidays with us. I also visited him in 1958 when I was eight years old (with my mom) at his home in Redwood City, where he lived with and was cared for by his youngest daughter, Veda Smith. I recall that Grandpa Smith was very old and in a wheelchair. He died that same year at the age of ninety-four.

Chapter 7: May Queen

I found this article in my grandmother's scrapbook. It was cut, pasted and very carefully saved from an account in the *Sacramento River News* from Friday, May 10, 1895. The article is signed "A Witness" but I have a suspicion that her mother, Marie Louise Anson Garrett, was the author.

Chapter 8: The Story of Josephine and Marcellus

My mother told me that her mother told her this story about the two nuns who suddenly left the convent of St. Gertrude's School. My grandmother concluded that they were together as a couple. My mother intimated that my grandmother felt a poignant sadness that they did not recognize and acknowledge my grandmother later on in all their lives. The names of Josephine and Marcellus are invented from the times.

Chapter 9: Lottie Moves to the City

From the stories my mother told me, I knew that my grandmother wanted to be an actress and that she met my grandfather at her Aunt Amy's boardinghouse at 610 Larkin, when she first came to San Francisco. When my mother Barbara passed away in 2016, I discovered that she had saved my grandparents' original wedding certificate from February 22, 1903 at St. Dominic's Church in San Francisco.

Chapter 10: Train Wreck

Of course, the front-page article about the train wreck, dated June 22, 1903 in the *San Francisco Examiner*, was saved in my grandmother's scrapbook. I discovered the scrapbook when I was about nine years old, and was surprised by the one-inch headlines screaming about a train wreck. It is startling to see it even now.

My mother didn't know why her parents were on that particular train, and at first, we thought they took the train to go on a picnic in the sunshine of Marin. However, in the spring of 2008 I went to the library in Tomales and discovered a book about local trains which explained that the train that crashed was a single-car train coming home from a funeral. I had to uncover facts about the funeral and put together clues as to why my grandparents were on that train, travelling home from Mr. Warren Dutton's funeral. Mr. Dutton had founded the town of Tomales and was one of the first to ship produce from Marin County to San Francisco. I am not certain why my grandparents were on that train, but I concluded from the newspaper accounts that there were business and friendship ties between Warren Dutton and my relatives Patrick Anson, Uncle Joe Cook, and Garrett Smith, all three of whom were in the business of shipping produce to San Francisco on the Bay's waters.

My mother did say that my grandmother had worn the brooch that day from her biological father, Benjamin Garrett, who had given it to her on the occasion of her high school graduation just the year before. The brooch was lost in the train wreck and never found. Facts from this story are based on eyewitness accounts in the San Francisco newspapers, the *Chronicle* and *Examiner*, dated after June 21, 1903, as well as the book *Narrow Gauge to the Redwoods* by A. Dickenson and R. Graves, published in 2008.

Chapter 11: 1906 Earthquake!

Ever since I was a child, I have heard stories of the big earthquake in San Francisco. By the time I was curious enough to ask about it, I was about nine years old and my maternal grandparents, Charlotte and Philip Lynch, had passed away. I knew that my paternal grandmother, Mary Cahill Mahoney, had lived through the 1906 San Francisco earthquake, and I asked her what she remembered. Occasionally, Grandma Mahoney stayed overnight at our home in the summertime. She had a thick Irish brogue and didn't say much about her past. But I remember sitting my nine-year-old self next to her on the couch in our Palo Alto living room, and her reply to my earthquake question is still clear in my mind. She said, "Oh, there was a lot of shaking! Buildings fell down, and I was all right, but many people were not." Mary Cahill was in her young twenties in 1906, and her Irish brogue carried a solemnity that I had not heard in an adult.

My mother knew these facts about her parents during the earthquake:

- ❖ Charlotte and Philip Lynch lived on Third and Clement Streets in San Francisco.
- ❖ My grandfather did rescue work with his team of horses.
- ❖ Their chimney and part of their ceiling collapsed. Yet all three of them—Philip, Charlotte and Walter, their baby—were physically unharmed.
- ❖ My aunt, Camilla Loughman, Barbara's sister, did indeed give the family photos of the earthquake to Goodwill, thinking that no one would be interested in them.

In May of 2012 I took a walking tour of the City with my brother, Pat Mahoney, to see the addresses and streets where our grandparents lived. Pat is a native San Franciscan who has lived in the City for more than forty years. When we went to Third and Clement, my brother pointed out that our grandfather would have wanted to check on his horses downtown, and could overlook downtown from the Laurel Street Hill Cemetery.

I had to refigure my grandfather's route for his rescue work. I assumed that he would take anyone who was hurt to the hospital nearest to his stable. I learned that there had been a makeshift hospital inside the large Mechanics Pavilion, which was two blocks away from his hay, grain and coal yard on 610 Larkin. However, at 1 pm, just eight hours after the initial quake, doctors and nurses were ordered to desert the Mechanics Pavilion with their patients because the roof was on fire. The building succumbed to flames that afternoon.

I learned this and many other facts from the combined *Call*, *Chronicle* and *Examiner* newspaper published the day after the earthquake. The Mechanics Pavilion was located at the current site of the Bill Graham Civic Auditorium at Grove and Larkin streets. Given this state of emergency that my grandfather witnessed, I imagined that he helped load his wagon with hospital patients and drove them to the hospital closest to his home, which would have been the Presidio Hospital near the Richmond District.

The rest of the historical facts were gleaned from many excellent books on the earthquake, and well-documented internet sites. One of the most helpful sites was the Bancroft Library site, which has published an interactive map of San Francisco's neighborhoods and photographs of the quake and fire. The interactive site is: http://bancroft.berkeley.edu/collections/earthquakeandfire/interactivemap/index.html

Chapter 12: The Taste of Sweet

Historical records from the Burlingame telephone book list Philip and Charlotte's address at 824 Acacia Drive, Burlingame.

My grandmother saved letters and newspaper articles in her scrapbook about the tea parties she hosted in Burlingame. In those days it was common for the local newspapers to publish short articles on get-togethers and women's afternoon tea parties. Recall that earlier chapters in this book tell the story of my grandmother's high school days and her "European education" from the French nuns at St. Gertrude's High School in Rio Vista. My grandmother grew up to enjoy the finer things in life that she witnessed at school and at home as a child. It was common in those days for women to have fine silver and china for serving afternoon tea. My mother saved my grandmother's china hot chocolate teapot for me. I proudly serve beverages with it in our home.

The *Crisco Cookbook* was published in 1915 by Procter and Gamble Co. to publicize their new invention of Crisco. I found it with my grandmother's things in our hall closet. I do have this cookbook in my possession now. It does easily open up to pages 122 and 123, labeled "Cakes." These pages bear the evidence of much of Charlotte's handiwork over the years. The pages hold imprints of sugar, cream and frosting, much to the delight of any reader or cook. My mother told me that her mother always made desserts, and there was something sweet on the table at the end of every meal.

Chapter 13: The Panama-Pacific International Exposition

Once again, my grandmother's scrapbook provided the basis for this story. Carefully pasted on one of the pages is a full map cut from a 1915 San Francisco newspaper showing the entire exhibition grounds. From this map, I intuited that my grandparents had visited this large and famous exhibition in their town, probably several times. I also have in my possession the fish platter that is referred to at the end of this chapter.

Many of the details in this chapter come from the book *San Francisco's Jewel City: The Panama-Pacific Exposition of 1915* by Laura A. Ackley, published in 2014.

Chapter 14: George Russell Lynch

For this chapter, I knew that my mother, her sister and brothers always said, "There were seven of us in our family." They always counted in their brother, Russell, as his memory never faded from their hearts. All of the Lynch siblings remembered as well that Russell's death "broke our mother's heart." I knew that Russell was buried with his toy fire engine, and it remains with him in the Holy Cross Cemetery in Colma, California, just south of San Francisco, to this day.

My grandmother carefully pasted the small article about Russell's death written by her neighbor, George Douglas, into her scrapbook of memories.

Chapter 15: Dust and Hope: Life on the Brentwood Farm

I visited the site of the Brentwood farm with my mother, my Uncle Phil Lynch, and my daughters, Katie and Emily Moorehead, in 1992. I had heard many times that my grandmother, who was heartbroken after Russell's death, did not take to the farm life at all. She was overwhelmed with the heat, the physical work of the farm, and the lack of city life.

You can visit the site of my great-grandfather Philip Lynch's farm today, as it was located right next to the current-day Shannon-Williamson Ranch Historical Park, 4900 Lone Tree Way, Antioch, CA 94509. On the Shannon-Williamson Ranch, there is a house and grounds with outbuildings that hold many artifacts from the early 1900s. It is owned by the State of California and has been designated a historical site.

Chapter 16: Lynch's Wild West Rodeo Show

This story is one that has been handed down in many forms. It is rather famous in our family annals and there are several different versions, depending on which uncle you talked to about it. I took the basis of the story from my cousin, Philip Lynch, who heard it from his father and uncles while duck hunting as a young boy, in the early morning light of the duck blinds on the Sacramento Delta.

Chapter 17: Lottie Employs her Talents

My mother told me that my grandmother kept herself busy and her mind sharp by driving the family Ford into town to take part in elocution and local plays in Brentwood and Antioch. There are small articles cut from the local newspapers and pasted in my grandmother's scrapbook that attest that she was a star performer in these local shows.

Chapter 18: The Gem

My grandfather is indeed listed in the 1922 San Francisco telephone directory as "Philip E. Lynch, Theater Manager, 973 Ocean Street, San Francisco." Facts about the family's jobs in this chapter were told to me by my mother and my Uncle Phil. Other facts are gleaned from my own research on the internet. The article on the Gem Theater's demise was pasted in my grandmother's scrapbook.

I learned other facts about silent movies from Professor Shelley Stamp at the University of California, Santa Cruz. Professor Stamp teaches classes in film, digital media and early movie history. She told me that it was not unusual for theaters in that time to burn, as film in those days was made of cellulose and were extremely combustible. Cellulose nitrate catches fire very easily, and once alight is difficult to put out. Fires involving cellulose nitrate burn extremely quickly with a hot, intense flame. Professor Sharp's website is http://film.ucsc.edu/faculty/shelley_stamp

From this information, I concluded that film combustion was the most likely cause of the fire. There was no insurance on the building, and bankruptcy once again entered my grandparents' lives.

Chapter 19: Capitola and San Francisco

This chapter is based on both oral and personal history. My mother told me most of the tales of her childhood: memories of sailing on the *Delta King*, living in San Francisco with her family, and tales of her early years as a young woman in the 1930s and 1940s. The Nakano Store is included in the Isleton section because of Fran Shimozaki, a friend I met on a Road Scholar boating trip in the Sacramento Delta. Fran told me that her grandfather, K. Nakano, had a dry goods store in Isleton at the same time that Veda lived there and Lottie and Barbara sailed to see the Smith family. Both of us felt that our ancestors had crossed paths in that small town, and that my great-aunt most likely purchased sewing notions and fabric from Mr. Nakano's store. Fran generously sent me the book *Delta Country* by Richard Dillon and Steve Simmons, which has excellent photographs and history of the Sacramento Delta lands.

I learned that Garrett Smith's ranch was purchased by Look Chong in the 1940s through an excellent website created by the descendants of the large Chinese community in the Delta. The Chong family's extensive historical research on their ancestors in the Delta can be found at:

http://w888.byethost32.com/ancestry/prt1/Ancestry.htm

This and other websites and histories are vital to our understanding of those times. Sadly, the Chinese and Japanese communities are often not fully included in written histories of these lands. I am grateful to Darryl Chong and Ronald Chong for giving permission to include a photo of the family that purchased the farm and ranch where my grandmother grew up.

My cousins, Patsy Smith, Nancy Basque, Sharon Bacigalupi, Philip Lynch, Donna Faulkner, Lorene Burnside, and Lois Pearse, and my siblings, Pat Mahoney and Sue Bowers, also contributed to these memories with fondness for their times spent with our grandparents.

Epilogue

The paintings of Charlotte Lynch are in the possession of many family members who recognize my grandmother's talent and eye for creating beautiful works of art. A few of the paintings are registered with the Smithsonian Inventory of American Paintings executed before 1914.

The Smithsonian website:

http://collections.si.edu/search/results.htm?date.slider=1900s,1910s&f.name.facet. prefix=G&facet.sort=false&q="Paintings"&fq=objecttype%3A"Paintings"&date.slid-er=1900s,1910s&fq=name:"Garret-Smith,+Charlotte"&list.name=&sl.id=

My grandmother's beautiful painting the "Fortune Teller" was painted when she was in high school. My mother loved this painting, and kept it prominently above her sofa in Santa Cruz. It is now in our family collection. It is based on a painting by Harry Roseland, who was known for paintings centered on African Americans of the early 1900s.

About the Author

Jean Mahoney was born in San Francisco and grew up in Palo Alto. She has studied San Francisco and the great Bay Area history for decades. Jean is a writer, poet and award-winning educator whose writing has appeared in the *Santa Cruz Sentinel* and *Sisters Singing*: *Blessings, Prayers, Art, Songs, Poetry and Sacred Stories by Women*. She taught sixth grade in public school in Santa Cruz for twenty years, and worked as a pioneer in environmental education and the movement for Life Lab school gardens. She later helped to design and present teacher training programs in the California Environmental Education Initiative curriculum. She lives in Santa Cruz, California.